THE EPICTETUS CLUB

THE
EPICTETUS
CLUB

BY
JEFF TRAYLOR
WITH INMATE ZENO

Papillon Press
Reprinted by:
Drinian Press, LLC

Direct inquiries to: EpictetusClub@ aol.com

ISBN-10: 0-941467-09-0
ISBN-13: 978-0-941467-09-4

Printed in the United States

To the former inmates on whom the characters Zeno, Doc, and Manny are based. Their success is a continuing reminder that change is possible for all of us.

THE EPICTETUS RAP

My name is Epictetus, here's what I'm puttin' down,
If you ain't got your cog skills, you're nothin' but a clown.
You know I was a prisoner, you know I was a slave,
It took all of my mind to control how I behave.
But I used my brain to live, I used my brain to get through,
I let go of entitlement, thinking I was due
Whatever I wanted, whatever anyone had,
I learned to focus elsewhere, then I didn't feel so bad.
I took my better feelings and opened up my mind,
I saw I used closed thinking, I saw that I was blind
To all my choices, all my options, all my possibility
And I made a vow right then that I knew I could be free
In my mind and in my heart
And in my thoughts is where to start.

So let me tell you what to do if you truly want to live
A life you can be proud of, a life where you can give
Instead of taking all the tim e, doing booze and drugs and
crime.
Clear your head, clear your conscience,
Clear your record, clear your mind,
Ain't no satisfaction in immediate grati-faction.

Now I know you think your circumstance
Is the reason for your victimstance,
But you know it ain't like that
You can survive like a cat.
Turn it on its ear, turn it upside down,
Instead of being crushed, ask how you can turn it 'round.
Don't just do the time, don't be a stupid fool,
This here is a place where if you play it cool,
You'll be stronger in your thinking, stronger in your heart,

When you come up out of here, you'll now know where to start
To live a life of purpose, to live the life you need,
To let go of your past, your demands and your greed.

Instead of robbin' in the hood, but sayin' you are good,
Get yourself on home, forget that Robin Hood syndrome.
Don't be makin' no excuses, don't be blamin' no one else,
Take responsibility and be Master of Yourself.

PREFACE

This novel is inspired by real events and real people. It is set in the old Ohio Penitentiary, and the descriptions of the institution are factual. Some events described as having taken place at the Ohio Penitentiary actually took place at Marion Correctional Institution. The inmate characters are fictional composites, and the names of staff have been changed. Epictetus (Epic-TEE-tus) was a real person.

My primary purpose when I began this book was to provide a refresher for the men who have completed a course in cognitive skills that I teach in a community-based correctional facility. By the time the men finish the course, they have studied many of these ideas, and this book is a practical and informative way for them to review the lessons as they prepare to return to society.

As the writing progressed, a second use for the book evolved - to provide these concepts and ideas to probationers or inmates at other correctional facilities who do not have access to these kinds of groups. Unfortunately, this is the vast majority of offenders. To you I say, "Welcome to the Epictetus Club, pull up a chair and enjoy the group – whether you are reading the book by choice or at the 'suggestion' of a judge or probation officer. In either case, I hope you find the lessons and discussions enjoyable and beneficial."

Of course, it would be preferable to have these skills taught to young people before they get into trouble, and many inmates have said that if they had learned these things in school, they would not have come to prison. The book can be used as a text in school reading programs, discussion groups, and even disciplinary programs, allowing students to develop thinking skills and reading skills at the same time.

A fourth purpose is to provide some ideas for the general reader who is interested in personal growth and change. While the stone walls of the penitentiary are real for the characters in the book, they also serve as a potent analogy for the rest of us as we struggle with our own limits and concerns.

Finally, the book provides a glimpse into a maximum-security prison – a place the vast majority of us, fortunately, has not seen. Whether the reader is just a curious citizen or a student considering a career in corrections, I hope to shed some light on these mysterious places and in the process dispel the notion that offenders are not interested in changing their lives for the better. While some offenders will indeed return to a criminal lifestyle, I know from countless personal experiences that many others will become productive and responsible members of society.

This is also an opportunity for me to acknowledge and thank the following people for giving me opportunities, inspiration, or support over the course of my career: Dr. Kimberly Zimmerman, Dr. Milt Cudney, Dr. Ross Mooney, Harold J. Cardwell, Pete Perini, Bruce Brunswick, Nancy Peteya, Rob Smith, Brian Moore, and Lisa DiSabato-Moore. I want to give a special thank you to my wife, who has been through it all with me, for her support of this book. Her creativity is a perpetual source of inspiration for me. Thank you one and all.

THE EPICTETUS CLUB

CHAPTER ONE

I first met the inmate they called Zeno shortly after starting my new job at the Ohio Penitentiary. I was 23 years old and fresh out of Ohio State. I had been hired to organize the furlough program at the prison, even though the ancient institution was slated for closing in six more months. "The Walls," as it was known to its residents, was a city within a city, home to several thousand maximum security inmates convicted of crimes ranging from robbery to murder. Its nickname came from the massive thirty-foot high, four-foot thick stone wall that completely surrounded the prison, sealing the inmates in and the world out. The wall had numerous guard towers along the top, manned by armed sharpshooters, as well as a tower in the center of the prison yard that oversaw the comings and goings of inmates and staff.

Inside the walls were several buildings, including Big Block, the cavernous cellblock that contained long ranges of cells stacked six stories high. The door to the cellblock was the same style as a barn door that had to be rolled aside, allowing cold winter winds and snow to blow into the block. Each cell held two bunk beds and four inmates, with a toilet sitting between the beds in the cramped quarters. Other buildings included C block (for close security), the cells for the most dangerous men and those on disciplinary restrictions. C block had gained public notoriety a few years earlier when the Ohio State Highway Patrol blew a hole in the wall and stormed into the block, ending a deadly prison riot. Along the same wall was D block, or Death Row.

The prison was built in the early 1800's and had housed prisoners dating back to the Civil War, including

1

John Morgan, whose soldiers had spread terror through Ohio during Morgan's Raid. Morgan would become the first and one of only a very few people to escape from the prison. Another famous "alumnus" was William Porter, whose pen name of O. Henry was literally a pen name, having been drawn from the words **Oh**io **Pen**it**e**ntia**ry**.

My office was located in the new section of the prison, built in 1878. To reach my office I had to pass through no fewer than six crash gates, those heavy iron-barred gates that would swing open and slam shut on heavy metal hinges. Creak-bang, creak-bang, creak-bang, creak-bang, creak-bang, creak-bang greeted me each morning as I made my way to the office. However, it was not necessary for me to wear myself out on the gates – they were opened and closed by stoic inmates whose job it was to stand at the gate and open and close it on the command of the gate officer. After finally passing through the final gate I would walk up a flight of stairs to the second floor classification department where my office was situated.

As the furlough counselor, I had a staff of several inmate clerk-typists, jobs that were highly coveted for their working conditions and lighter work. They sure beat the coal pile. The inmates in our department had an occasional opportunity to sit and talk with the counselors and staff, so we came to know each other fairly well. One day I overheard one of my clerks telling another inmate, "Mr. Traylor should meet Zeno – they would have a hell of a conversation." When I asked him why he said that, he sheepishly apologized and said that he only meant that Zeno and I shared a love for "deep stuff." I laughed it off, and asked who Zeno was. "You don't know Zeno? He's the guy that opens the last gate for you every morning. I think his real name is Richard, but the inmates call him Zeno."

2

The next day at the gate I formally introduced myself to Zeno. He appeared to be in his mid-forties, about six-feet tall with short cropped gray hair, blue-gray eyes, and a lean, muscular build. I told him that another inmate had suggested that I might enjoy a conversation with him because we both liked "deep stuff." We shared a laugh, and Zeno said that he would be happy to talk with me any time. He invited me to stop by his "lock" (prison slang for an inmate's living quarters), but it would be a couple more weeks before I was able to do so. I can honestly say that I have never had a conversation in a more unusual place – the Death House at the Ohio Penitentiary.

CHAPTER TWO

At first I thought he was kidding – surely no one "locked" in the Death House. But that is where Zeno said he lived. I had seen the Death House every day that I went to work – it was a small brick building that sat in the prison yard not far from Zeno's gate. Inside was the electric chair, Ohio's instrument of ultimate punishment. It had not been used for nine years.

As I entered the little building Zeno greeted me cordially. I was immediately impressed with his calm and self-assured demeanor. He had a serenity about himself that was all the more remarkable for being in such a setting. When he walked across the room to greet me, I noticed a slight limp. "An old injury from my younger days," he said as he reached out to shake hands. He asked me if I had ever been inside the Death House, and I told him that I had not. He offered to give me a tour.

As it turned out, Zeno was somewhat of an authority on the death penalty. Of course, the most prominent feature in the room was the electric chair, which sat on a platform about eight inches high. It was roped off with velvet ropes similar to those seen in bank lines. But the most eerie feature of the room was the hundreds of photos lining the walls – photos of the men and women who had died in the electric chair over the years. Zeno described the stories of several of the people in the pictures, including the story of the man who had helped develop the leg holds while serving a prison sentence, only to be later returned to prison for murder and executed in the very chair he helped design. When we reached the last photo, Zeno paused and pointed at the blank space to the right of the photo of Donald Reinbolt and said, "That is where my photo was to hang, but I received a last minute

4

commutation that spared my life. After that, I was given the job of maintaining the Death House, and this is where I live." All he had was a cot, a couple of books on a small stand, and of course, the photos.

I admit that I was somewhat shaken by what I had just seen, and Zeno picked up on it when he asked me if I was all right. "Aren't you upset by living in here in the midst of all this death?" I asked, thinking that this must surely rank as some form of cruel and unusual punishment.

He calmly replied, "If I told myself, 'this is awful, death is scary, and they shouldn't do this to me,' I would feel just as you do – shook up. But I'm not. You see a Death House, but I see a hermitage. I have the only private quarters in the penitentiary, and I appreciate my privacy and time to read and study in solitude. I've learned that it is our view of things, rather than the things themselves, that upsets us. We can stop and try to see things from another angle, from a point that is more beneficial for us. Perhaps it is your *view* that death is scary and awful that upsets you, not these photos and chair. *If you change what you tell yourself about something, you will change your response to it.*"

I was interested in the idea that it is our view that upsets us, but I was also concerned that his attitude toward death was one that allowed him to minimize his own crime, and he again picked up on my thoughts. "I committed a murder when I was twenty-five years old. I was young and hot-blooded and got into a fight over a girl. There is no excuse for what I did, and I regret it every day of my life. I know that I cannot undo the damage I caused, but there is something I *can* do – and I am doing it. That is how I can go on with my life."

Before I could ask him what that something was, the prison horn sounded for dinner. Zeno had to join his company to march to the dining hall, so we cut short our conversation. I asked him if we could continue our talk next Friday, and he readily agreed. As I walked out of the Death House, I looked up to the sky, and took a deep breath of fresh air.

CHAPTER THREE

I had been thinking about what Zeno said at our last meeting – *that people were not upset by things themselves, but by what they told themselves about those things.* At first I had my doubts. But I was also open to considering it, so I decided to pay attention to my thoughts the next time I was worried, upset or angry. It didn't take long to find my first opportunity. Driving home that evening after work, someone cut me off on the freeway, and then had the nerve to give me the "we're number one" sign. My instant reaction was to think, "Who the hell does he think he is? I'm going to pull up beside him and tell him a thing or two." Then I thought of what Zeno had said, and tried something new. I told myself, "That guy is obviously having a bad day, and I don't need to make him a part of my day. I'll just take a deep breath and go on listening to the radio." To my amazement, and just as Zeno predicted, my feeling about the situation changed from anger to minor annoyance and then to complete indifference about the other guy. I felt more in control of my feelings and actions than I ever had! I couldn't wait to talk with Zeno again.

When Friday rolled around, I stopped by Zeno's House (I preferred thinking about it that way) for our chat and found him reading a little book with the strange title *Enchiridion*. He promptly laid it down on his stand, and it was then that I noticed a snapshot in a matchstick frame sitting on the stand. In the photo one could see Zeno smiling broadly, surrounded by boxing promoter Don King, former heavyweight champion Joe Louis and someone I didn't recognize. Zeno explained that the photo had been taken about a year earlier when Don King brought ABC Wide World of Sports to the prison to televise some professional bouts on national TV. King's entourage

7

included Joe Louis, one of America's greatest heroes, and an unknown young boxer named Larry Holmes. "Don told me to be sure to get Larry in the picture. I didn't know who he was, but Don said that he would one day be the heavyweight champion of the world, so Larry was kind enough to get into the photo with me. We'll see if Don was right or just blowing smoke from one of his big cigars!"

Zeno paused to look at the photo, and then said that he used to do some professional boxing in Akron. "At the time I didn't know how important that would be to helping me survive in the pen, but it has literally saved my life."

"How many fights have you been in with other inmates?" I asked.

"At first, a lot, but none for the past ten years." he said with a wry smile. "My boxing skills now help me avoid that kind of trouble."

He went on to ask if I remembered what he had said about the importance of our thoughts, and I described to him my incident of road rage on the freeway and how I had calmed myself down just by changing what I was telling myself.

"You'd probably be a good boxer," he said. "Thinking skills and boxing skills are very similar. Think of yourself as in a boxing ring with an opponent, but your opponent is not another person – your opponent is your own thinking. There are some thoughts that can take you out for the count, like your thought of 'Who the hell does he think he is?' I see it all the time in here. Of course, the thought that has knocked out nearly everyone here is 'I won't get caught.'"

He laughed, and went on. "A good boxer is able to recognize and anticipate what his opponent is going to do, is able to recognize the punch that is coming, block it, then throw a counterpunch. In our thinking, if we can recognize self-defeating thoughts as they come up, block them, and then respond with a productive counterpunch, we can avoid trouble and live a good life. If we can't do that, we will have a life of pain and turmoil. But just like in boxing, it takes practice, practice, practice. Good thinking is not a haphazard enterprise, or something that some are born with and some are not."

"Are you saying that thinking well is not a question of intelligence, but a matter of skill?" I asked.

"Exactly. And it is also a question of bravery."

"Bravery?"

"Yes, bravery. The ancient Greeks said that learning to think well is a moral virtue they called courage, because it takes commitment and effort. They also said that those who do not take pains to learn to think clearly are committing the moral vice of cowardice. Just as someone on a battlefield who runs away out of fear of getting hurt is a coward, so are people who refuse to take the necessary pains to change their lives also cowards. Those who *do* take the pains and effort are demonstrating courage, just as much as the person on the battlefield who overcomes fear of injury and fights for a good cause."

"How does one develop these skills?"

"The way we do it in here is to get together at the Epictetus Club."

"The Epictetus Club? What's that?"

"It's a group of inmates who meet once a week. We are open to everybody who would like to come, regardless of age, race, religion, or criminal offense – or even whether you are an inmate or staff member. The prison chaplain is our staff advisor, but he mostly just provides the space for us to meet on Friday nights. I like to think of it as Friday

1. Don't anchor yourself
1. to one self

2.

3.

4.

9
5.

Night at the Fights – but our fights are with our own thoughts and attitudes. Remember, thinking is like boxing - identify the thought, block it, and counterpunch. Speaking of the Epictetus Club, I better start getting ready for the meeting. Have a good weekend and I'll see you Monday at the gate."

CHAPTER FOUR

I like to spend time browsing through used bookstores, and over the weekend I stopped by Hoffman's Books in Columbus. I was looking through the Ohio history section when I noticed a thin pamphlet-like book stuck between two others. I pulled it out and was stunned to see that it was a copy of the *Enchiridion*! I remembered that this was the same small book that Zeno had on his stand when I visited him the previous week. Not only does the book not have a printed spine, which made it nearly invisible, but it was also out of place - the *Enchiridion* had nothing to do with Ohio history. This is beyond coincidence, I thought, as I took it to the register. Ed Hoffman said that he had bought a collection of Ohio books at an estate auction a few days earlier and apparently the book was in that stack. A mere 29 pages long and saddle-stitched, it was not exactly an impressive-looking tome. "Give me a buck and its yours," he said. I happily paid for the booklet and took it home.

Almost half of the book was devoted to an introduction, and I soon found out why Zeno's group called itself the Epictetus Club. Epictetus was a philosopher who lived about 2,000 years ago during the Roman Empire, and he had been born a slave and a prisoner. As a young boy an especially cruel master had crippled him, and he spent the rest of his life lame and suffering ill health. Nevertheless he used his experiences to make himself stronger, kinder, and wiser instead of bitter and angry. He was eventually granted his freedom as a young man and began teaching principles of personal freedom and tranquility. He developed such a large following that he and other philosophers were deemed a threat by the Roman emperor. He anticipated Thoreau, Gandhi, and King by refusing to shave off his beard to show the public his subservience to the emperor. Under threat of beheading he essentially said, "I won't shave. I never said I was immortal or couldn't lose my head. You do what you have to do and I'll do what I have to do – and that is to live according to my nature and purpose." He was then exiled to the coast of Greece where he ran a small school teaching how to live a life of serenity and purpose by mastering one's desires, performing one's duties, and knowing one's relationship to the big picture. He was said to be a kind and good-hearted man, passing away around the year 130 A.D at the age of 80. He wrote nothing himself, but one of his students feverishly took notes during the lectures. These notes were to become the *Discourses of Epictetu s*, and the *Enchiridion* just included the highlights of the eight books that comprised the *Discourses* – what amounted to the world's first *Cliff Notes*.

Enchiridion means "handbook" and through this handbook the wisdom of Epictetus was passed down through the centuries. His teachings were admired by Marcus Aurelius, perhaps the greatest warrior-emperor of the Roman Empire, and Frederick the Great, who would not leave on a military campaign without a copy of the *Enchiridion* in his pack. Vietnam War fighter pilots studied the handbook in case they were shot down and taken prisoner. I could easily see how Epictetus would be of enormous value to people confined in a prison, and I was excited about how his teachings could also be applied to my own life. After all, who isn't interested in personal freedom and tranquility in the midst of strife and stress?

Monday morning as I passed through the last gate Zeno said, "Good book, isn't it?" I then realized that my copy of the *Enchiridion* was sticking out of my stack of papers.

"I read the whole thing over the weekend," I replied, and we both laughed.

"Now you know why we call our group the Epictetus Club. We help each other apply some of the ideas taught by Epictetus. Feel free to stop by sometime – but you probably have better things to do on a Friday night," he laughed.

"Thanks for the invitation. I'll think about it," I replied, just before the gate slammed shut with its characteristic bang.

CHAPTER FIVE

The week passed uneventfully – for a maximum-security prison, anyway. I hadn't seen Zeno since Monday, since he had been assigned to a special outside detail. Zeno was a trusted inmate with honor status, which meant that he could go outside the prison walls under guard for special duties. That week the honor contingent was doing some work on a state building downtown a few blocks away. Now it was Friday afternoon, and Zeno was back on the gate. We exchanged pleasantries as I was leaving for the day, and I wished him a good meeting of the Epictetus Club that evening.

"There is no meeting tonight," he said.

"Why not?"

"The chaplain was offered a job at another prison and he took it, naturally. Without a staff advisor inmates aren't allowed to gather, so it looks like our group may be finished."

The Ohio Penitentiary was in its long, slow decline toward extinction. At its height, it housed more than 5,000 inmates, but the number was declining daily. A new modern maximum-security prison had just been built in Lucasville, and the transfer of inmates from Columbus to the Southern Ohio Correctional Facility was underway. The process was a major undertaking shrouded in secrecy. Inmates were on a be-ready-to-go-at-any-time basis, and no one except a few administrators and those in the classification department knew who would be transferred until it was time for the inmate to grab his few possessions and get on the bus. That way it would be difficult for anyone to plan an escape by having accomplices on the outside lying in wait along the route to Lucasville. In addition to the internal secrecy, there were other precautions. Heavily armed State Highway Patrol officers in cruisers were stationed in front of and behind the bus, and a helicopter flew overhead for the entire trip. Local police and sheriff's deputies joined the caravan as it passed through each of their jurisdictions, creating a surreal parade through many small Ohio towns.

Staff members were also disappearing as they were reassigned to other facilities or simply quit to pursue other interests and careers. Corrections work seems to be something that you are either cut out to do or you are not. The retiring Institution Parole Officer whom I was replacing told me on my first day that after a while you have correction fluid flowing through your veins instead of blood. I laughed and thought he was kidding. Now I'm not so sure.

"I'm sorry about your group," I told Zeno.

"Thanks, but all things must pass. Have a good weekend."

This was a very uncharacteristic response from an inmate. My admittedly brief tenure at the prison had taught me that most of the time when an inmate did not get his way there would be yelling, pouting, threats of lawsuits, or the familiar "this is bullshit!" But here was Zeno calmly wishing me a nice weekend after he had lost something that was of central importance to him.

"I must say, you seem to be taking it very well, Zeno."

"Of course I'm disappointed, but these are the times where you can strengthen yourself. Who can't handle it when things are going smoothly and you are getting what you want? The challenge is to maintain your balance when things aren't going so well. That is what Epictetus taught. Do you remember the first words in the *Enchiridion*?"

"Not exactly," I replied as I searched my memory to no avail.

"'Some things are up to us, and some things are not up to us.' That is probably the forerunner of the Serenity Prayer. If you can correctly sort events into one of those two piles, you have a very good chance of being happy and efficient. If you sort poorly or put your attention onto the wrong pile, you will be angry and frustrated. For example, it is not up to me if the chaplain leaves, so why should I get upset about it, whine about the unfairness of it all, or complain to others about it? That is his business, and I would do just what he did if I was in his shoes. I have to look beyond my own desires to the big picture. Can I change him or that circumstance? No. What *is* up to me is my own response to the situation, my own attitude, and my own thoughts. Why give myself a needless headache? I have my hands full with the stuff that *is* up to me, so that is where I'll place my energy and attention. The best course for me is to let it go, be happy that I had it at all, and move on. Besides, things will work out just as they are supposed to if I don't get in the way."

"That certainly seems to make sense. You obviously walk the talk, Zeno. Still, I'm sorry about the Club. I'll see you Monday."

"If I'm not on the bus before then," he laughed. "And thanks for your kind words, Mr. Traylor."

As the gate slammed behind me, I remember thinking that maybe there was something to this Epictetus Club after all.

***

Monday morning I headed straight for the warden's office, which was located near the main entrance, before going to the classification department. I had met the warden

16

briefly only once, having been interviewed for my job by the assistant warden and the social services director. Warden Cartwright was already in the office that morning, and his secretary buzzed me through to see him. Before I could tell him who I was, he was admonishing me for some of the candidates who were being considered for furlough. I was surprised that he knew who I was, and even more taken aback by the upbraiding. He did say that he liked the procedures I had developed, though.

"Thank you," I replied, thinking about how to get better quality maximum-security inmates to release on furlough.

"What can I do for you?" he asked.

"I understand that the chaplain has resigned and is transferring to another prison."

"That's right. Do you want to be the chaplain? You kind of look like a shepherd," he said, and then laughed. I figured he was referring to my long hair, and I could feel myself getting annoyed at his criticism of both my work and my appearance. I went on to explain that I had been thinking about taking over as advisor of one of the chaplain's groups, specifically the Epictetus Club.

"The Epictetus Club? Why that one?"

"Well, the inmates need an advisor to continue their meetings, and I am interested in the topic, so I thought it might be a good match for everyone."

He swiveled in his chair to look out the window behind his desk, turned back around and said, "I don't see any problem with you being an advisor. And to be honest, we have fewer problems with those men than with any others, so I would like to see the group continue. Some of the corrections officers are a little suspicious though, since those Epictetus guys are always so hard to rattle and hardly ever get to enjoy the hospitality of a correction cell." Correction cell was the polite term for "the hole," where disruptive and unruly inmates were sent for up to 15 days at a time. The hole was a dark, dungeon-like affair, and at night the inmate in one of these solitary confinement cells might enjoy the company of a large rodent if he forgot to line up his shoes and clothing at the bottom of the cell door.

I was particularly interested to learn that the "Epictetus guys" were not easily provoked by the few guards who seemed to enjoy tormenting the prisoners. In prison parlance, apparently the Epictetus guys were not "easily played." I thanked the warden for his time and turned to go, but before I reached the door he called out to me.

"There is one problem. We don't have any space for your meetings. As we close each section of the prison, it is sealed off to conserve heat and manpower. If you can find a space that won't cost us anything, go ahead."

I headed off to my office, and encountered Zeno at the last gate. "Good morning," he said.

"Morning," I grumbled, before I caught myself and forced a smile.

"Looks like you might have something on your mind," he said.

"I just came from the warden's office," I said, and before I could tell him the news about the club, he guessed that I must have had a difficult meeting.

"Did you just have your initiation?" he asked with a big smile on his face.

"What are you talking about?"

"Did he say anything critical about you?"

"I don't know that that is really something I want to discuss with you."

Now he was smiling even more broadly. "The warden and I have known each other for many years, and one thing that I have noticed consistently is that he will test new inmates and employees by either insulting them or criticizing them when they first meet. He watches to see their reactions, and that tells him a lot about the man's self-control and future at this facility. How did you do?"

"It depends on how perceptive he is," I answered, and we both laughed. "If he is as perceptive as you are, I didn't do all that well."

"We have to deal with that stuff all the time in here. The way I stay out of the hole when someone tries to play me is to remember the rock example from Epictetus."

"The rock example?"

"Epictetus said something like, 'what is this nonsense about being insulted or disrespected? Try to insult a rock and see what happens.' What he means is that you will only look foolish. So when someone is trying to insult or provoke you, listen like a rock. Don't react in a haphazard or impulsive way. Stay calm and centered. That way you keep your own power instead of giving it away to the other person. The insulter ends up looking foolish, just like the person who insults a rock. The defensiveness of the insulted is the insulter's only advantage, and if you listen like a rock you don't get defensive and you don't get played."

"That sounds like good advice, Zeno. I did talk with the warden about the Epictetus Club. I have some good news and some bad news. I asked to be the advisor for the Club, and he said I could be."

"Is that the good news or the bad news?" Zeno joked.

19

"I think that is the good news, but I'm not sure. The bad news is that there is no space to hold the meetings since the meeting room in the chapel building is being closed off. The warden said if I could find a meeting place that didn't cost the state anything we could go ahead with the Epictetus Club."

"No problem," Zeno immediately replied. "We can meet in the Death House. It has to be heated anyway, so that meets that hurdle. I don't mind being the host, either. That way I won't have to cross the yard on cold winter nights!"

So it was agreed upon, and approved by the warden, that the new meeting place for the Epictetus Club was officially the Death House. What would Epictetus have thought about that, I wondered.

CHAPTER SIX

When the passes went out Friday morning for the day's appointments, there were a lot of puzzled looks among both the inmates and corrections officers. No one had ever received, or even seen, a pass to the Death House. I imagine there was some reluctance on the part of a few inmates to honor the pass, although the honoring of passes was mandatory. As the day wore on and word spread that I had sent the passes, the joke became that I was running a hell of a furlough program and that the number of requests for consideration was sure to drop! I imagined the satisfaction that that would bring to the warden.

I arrived for the meeting promptly at 7:00 PM and began by introducing myself to the dozen men who had gathered for the Epictetus Club meeting. As I did so, Zeno and I exchanged quick glances, asking nonverbally if the other knew where the chair and photos had gone, but neither of us had a clue. The walls were blank except for the outlines where the picture frames had hung just hours ago, and the platform that held the electric chair was also empty. The answers would have to wait, though, since it was time to get started.

I was one of three new faces at the meeting. The prison grapevine is faster than fiberoptic cable, so everyone already knew that I was the new club advisor – and also the new furlough counselor. Each man seemed acutely aware that my job was to screen suitable candidates for early release on furlough and forward their names to the parole board for final determination. Naturally, everyone was very polite and courteous.

After all the men introduced themselves to me and handed me their passes, I turned the meeting over to Zeno and sat down outside of the circle. Zeno began by thanking

21

me for offering to be the advisor, and suggesting to the men that they not use the meeting as an excuse to lobby for furlough. "Send a kite to Mr. Traylor if you want to discuss furlough, and he'll take care of it during regular business hours. None of us are here for that on Friday nights." That was the last mention of furlough at any of the club meetings.

Zeno went on to describe the group rules, which were few and simple: respect your fellow group members by paying attention when they speak, only one person speaks at a time, and what is said in the meeting stays in the meeting. He then gave some background on the Epictetus Club for the benefit of the new members and myself.

The Club had been meeting for about five years, and had been started by Zeno and another inmate named Doc. Doc was not actually a doctor, but had been a medic in the army before coming to the penitentiary on a second-degree murder conviction. Doc had served ten years at the Walls and had been transferred to the medium security Marion Correctional Institution a little over two years ago, leaving Zeno to organize and lead the groups himself. It was actually Zeno who had first discovered the teachings of Epictetus and tried them out.

"When I first came to the Walls, I had what you might call a bad attitude," he began. "I was angry and bitter and facing a death sentence, and when that was commuted, I was still facing a life sentence. I had been a boxer, so after I came off the Row I was being challenged to a lot of fights in here. And I felt like I had to answer every challenge. Today I see that I was being played and was the entertainment for the instigators, since I would keep getting sent to the hole. After one fifteen-day stint in the hole I had been reassigned to a new cell as part of my punishment –

the cell on the first tier in Big Block right by the door. That is the cell that ends up with the snowdrifts in it during the winter when the wind blows the snow through those big doors.

"When I entered my new cell, I immediately searched it for contraband that may have been left by the previous tenant. I did not want to go back to the hole for someone else's stuff. I tossed the mattress, and underneath it was a skinny little book called *The Enchiridion: The Handbook of Epictetus*. I opened it up and at random I read the passage that said "set up a certain character and pattern for yourself which you will preserve when you are with people and when you are alone. Be silent for the most part and say what you have to say in a few words. Don't be afraid of verbal abuse or criticism. If someone comes up to you and says so-and-so is saying bad things about you, don't get upset and react, but instead say 'apparently that person doesn't know me very well if those are the only bad things he had to say about me.'

"I couldn't believe it. It was as if that book had been placed there just for me. That paragraph I found at random addressed my main problem. I could see that this guy Epictetus was the real deal, and I devoured the rest of the book that night. In the years since then, I have not been back to the hole a single time, and I have more personal freedom and peace inside here than I ever did outside, which just proves another of Epictetus's points: you can make your life a prison or a palace just by how you think.

"Some time later I told my friend Doc about the book, and he said that he knew some pilots in the army who studied Epictetus in case they were shot down and taken POW. He was interested in it so we started studying it together, and soon someone else wanted to join us, and it finally grew into the Epictetus Club. But that is enough about the club history and me. I am happy that you are all here tonight and I hope that you find what you are looking for. Let's go around and introduce ourselves to each other."

One by one the regular members stated their names and welcomed the newcomers. After the two new men introduced themselves to the group, Zeno rolled out a chalkboard on wheels that had been requisitioned from the old meeting room in the chapel. "We have a little brain teaser for the new guys in the group, and it helps get us all on the same page quickly." He then drew nine dots on the blackboard, three dots in three rows, forming a square, and asked the two new guys to connect all nine dots with four straight lines without lifting the chalk from the board. I drew the dot diagram on a piece of paper and quietly tried it myself as the new guys struggled with the solution.

*   *   *

*   *   *

*   *   *

About a minute after we started working on the puzzle, an intimidating-looking group member they called Animal said he wanted to help, and he started telling a story about a couple of frogs.

"Once upon a time there was a frog who lived in a dark, dank well. One day this frog was visited by a frog from the ocean. After the frog from the ocean jumped down into the well, the frog in the well said, 'Where are you from?'

'Oh, I'm from the ocean,' the visitor replied.

'How big of a place is that?" asked the frog in the well.

'Oh, it's gigantic,' said the frog from the ocean.

'Is it a fourth as big as my well?' asked the frog in the well.

'It's bigger than that.'

'Is it half as big as my well?"

'Bigger.'

'Is it as big as my well?'

'It's bigger than your well. It's huge!' said the frog from the ocean.

'I don't believe it,' said the frog in the well. 'You'll have to show me!'

So the frog from the ocean took the frog from the well to see the ocean, and when the frog from the well saw the ocean, his head exploded into a thousand pieces."

The new guys looked at Animal like he was out of his mind, and I wondered what I had gotten myself into. He then said, "Relax, it's part of the puzzle. It's a clue that will make sense in a minute."

After a couple more minutes passed, the guys gave up, with one of them saying the puzzle couldn't be solved. I couldn't figure it out either, even with the help of the frog story, but fortunately no one noticed me struggling with it.

"Don't feel bad," a group member named Eddie told the new guys. "No one has ever been able to do it at the first meeting, including us." He then demonstrated the solution.

"Oh, man! That was so easy, I can't believe I didn't get it!" exclaimed the man who said it couldn't be done.

"What did you guys do that kept you from solving the puzzle?" asked Eddie.

"We stayed inside the box," they both agreed.

"That demonstrates how our thinking works," said Zeno. "We only go to the edge of our old thinking, and either give up, or don't think there is any other way to think. As a result, we stay in the box and don't come up with the solutions to our problems. Maybe you've heard that old phrase, 'If you always do what you've always done, you'll always get what you've always got'. This prison with its four stone walls is definitely a box, and if we don't change the way we think, we'll either never get out of this box, or if we do get out, we'll keep coming back."

"I see what you're saying," said one of the new guys. "But what does the frog have to do with it?"

Animal was eager to share the meaning of his story. "The frog in the well represents us when we are using our old thinking that limits us and causes us trouble. This old penitentiary is definitely a dank, dark well. After a while, though, we think that this is all there is. The wall helps make that happen by screening out everything from the outside world. But one day a frog from the ocean hops into the well, and the frog in the well learns that there is more to life than what he sees in the well. After he sees that, his head explodes into a thousand pieces. That means that his old way of thinking is shattered, he has a broader vision of life and a bigger purpose."

"That's a good story, but I have a question. How could the frog really think that his well was any bigger than a little ol' well?" asked the second of the new guys.

"It happens when we get used to our environment and eventually we think it is more common or normal than it is – more spacious. Let me ask you a question: What percentage of people in the state of Ohio do you think are incarcerated?"

The other man thought for a moment, then asked if that included all state prisons, all county jails, and other confinement facilities. "If you count all of them, then, I would say about 30%," he finally answered with an air of authority.

"Your answer is typical – when I ask that question of other inmates, the answers consistently range from 20% to 70%. I myself answered 40% the first time I was asked that question. We think our well is a lot bigger than it is – but only one out of every 142 people is incarcerated. That is less than one percent. If I was a gambling man, I could have made a lot of money on that question," he said with a sly smile as he cast a look in my direction. "When each of those ones are thrown together in the same place, it looks to us like everyone is a criminal or thinks like one. We need to think outside the box if we want to live outside the box, and realize that life is a lot more than what we see inside these walls. There is another way to think that creates a life beyond this prison, and we can start creating it even while we are in here. Think of it as going to the ocean," he said with a laugh.

After a bit more discussion, the hour was up and it was time for the inmates to return to their locks for count. Zeno said that the next session would be devoted to getting past the walls – the walls in our minds, he was quick to add for my benefit. Everyone then hurried out, since missing count was a serious infraction. I felt good about the meeting and was impressed with the men. I was thinking about the similarities of how Zeno and I both came across our copies of the book, and about my own "well" and how I could broaden my own horizons. As I made my way through the gates to the main entrance, I walked past the warden as he was locking his door. He asked about the meeting, and said that he hoped we had enough chairs. "I took the liberty of removing one of them and shipping it to Lucasville. Ol' Sparky can be a little distracting." He smiled and bade me good night.

CHAPTER SEVEN

I arrived a few minutes early for the next meeting, having stayed in the institution between the end of the workday and the start of the meeting in order to catch up on some paperwork. The first thing I noticed when I entered the room was a frame hanging on the wall in the same spot where a photo of one of the executed prisoners had hung. But there was no photo in the frame – just some words. As I walked up to look at it, I could see that it was a neatly written small poster that said:

Round One
ABC's of Inner Boxing
<u>A</u>ttacking Thought:
Identify the self-defeating thoughts you are using in the situation

<u>B</u>lock the Attacking Thought:
Ask "is this thought true? Where does this thought lead? Is that where I want to go?"

<u>C</u>ounterpunch:
Replace the attacking thought with a productive thought

"Don't worry, it's not mushfake," said Zeno.

"It's not what?" I asked.

"You really are new, aren't you!" he answered. "Mushfake means to alter or destroy state property, such as using state materials like wood to make these frames. It's against the rules. But I found the pile of frames in the storage closet where I keep my cleaning supplies, without the photos. Those have apparently gone to the historical society. I asked if I could use the frames for the Epictetus Club, and the warden said it was okay."

"Actually, I was more interested in what is *in* the frame than the frame itself."

Just then the group members began arriving, so I took my seat and collected the passes. One member was not present, so I said, "I hope he didn't get in trouble for mushfaking."

Everyone looked at me with a puzzled expression, but Zeno laughed, knowing I was just trying out my new word – an early foray into learning prisonese.

"No, he's not in trouble, he went on sick call."

The meeting began with Zeno comparing the thinking skills that Epictetus taught to the boxing skills he had learned as a professional boxer. He pointed to the frame and said that he planned to add a new frame each week or so, and that he would be open to any suggestions that anyone might have as to what to put in it. He then introduced what he called the ABC model of Inner Boxing. *A* represented what he termed the *attacking thought*, which is the self-defeating thought that arises and attacks us, causing emotional upheaval, ineffective solutions or trouble; *B* represented the *blocking* of the attacking thought, usually by asking the questions "is this thought true? Where does it lead? Is that where I want to go in the long run?" The *C* represents the *counterpunch*, the thought that you could tell yourself instead, thereby neutralizing or obliterating the attacking thought.

"First, identify the attacking thought that you are throwing at yourself; second, block it with the key questions; third, counterpunch it with a better, more effective thought. It is just like being in the ring, but your opponent is your own thoughts and attitudes. Epictetus warns us to be on guard against ourselves as an enemy lying in wait. You are not likely to meet a more formidable opponent than yourself. I've fought some middle weight contenders for the crown in my time, and none of them was as tricky or as fast as my own mind!" he said with earnestness. "If you really want to prove yourself, take on your own thoughts instead of blaming someone else for your emotions. That is being a real warrior instead of a playground bully. Getting into a physical fight or throwing a verbal punch at someone else means that you have already lost the main bout – the one with yourself. Everything else is just the undercard."

He then asked Shakes, the inmate who last week thought the puzzle couldn't be solved, if he would like to do some sparring using the ABC example in the frame.

Shakes readily agreed to try it. "Last week, I said that the nine-dots puzzle couldn't be solved and I gave up. The Attacking Thought I used was, 'It can't be done.' Instead of just quitting, I could have identified the thought as a self-defeating, attacking thought and blocked it by asking, 'Is that true?' I didn't know if it was or not, so I shouldn't have assumed that it was. 'Where does this thought lead?' It leads to giving up, not solving the problem, and feeling frustrated. 'Is that where I want to go?' No, it isn't. Therefore, it is in my best interest to throw a counterpunch, such as 'Think outside the box, see the problem from another angle.'"

"Great job, Shakes. I see a warrior-in-training here. When we used the counterpunch thought of 'think outside the box,' we solved the puzzle and we won the round. One round does not win the fight, but if you build up enough rounds you *will* win the fight. It takes a steady effort over time, but you will begin to see progress if you stick with it. Our goal is not perfection, but progress. You will lose a round now and then, or get knocked down, but just get back up and get back in the fight. You don't lose until you don't get back up."

We then moved on to the night's scheduled topic: how we keep ourselves in the box. "In the pen it seems obvious what keeps us in here – a 30-foot high stone wall with guard towers. But what keeps us in the box or in the well of our own mind? What keeps us from growing as much as we could, or from having the life we want, inside or outside of a prison?" He again drew the nine-dot diagram on the board, and drew four lines around it. "Each line represents one of the things that keeps us from going outside the well of our old, self-defeating thinking: fear, apathy, inertia, and lack of a vision. There is an easy way to remember these four obstacles: the first letter of each word spells out F.A.I.L."

Fear

Lack of Vision

Apathy

Inertia

"These are the four walls that keep us confined just as much, if not more, than the stone walls you see around us. As inmates we all know what will happen if we walk toward a wall, so we don't even consider it after a while. We might even forget the walls are there and adapt to our small world. Likewise, we get so used to the comfort of our old thinking that we don't even consider changing, and we adapt to the negative consequences we have accumulated. But when we wake up to these consequences and decide to leave the well, we find out what our obstacles are when we start to make our move. You will hear the guards in your mind lock and load."

After a short pause in the conversation, Animal spoke up, saying that he was reminded of another story about a frog. It began to dawn on me that Animal's nickname came not from his fearsome looks but from his animal stories. "When you make frog soup, if you put a frog in hot water it will jump out, but if you put a frog in cold water and slowly turn up the heat you can cook it. The frog gradually adapts to the increasing temperatures until it is cooked – and it sounds like you are saying that we do the same thing."

"That's right," replied Zeno. "As a child, do you remember setting the goal for yourself of becoming a criminal and going to prison?"

"Of course not, but I can see now how it happened. I got in trouble at home, then adapted. I went to juvey, and then adapted. I went to the county for a while, then I adapted. Then I went to state prison, and here I am adapting again. I'm cooking myself one step at a time, until I'm frog soup!"

The other men nodded in agreement as they thought back on their own lives.

"You are today where your thoughts have brought you, and you will be tomorrow where your thoughts take you – one thought at a time," said Zeno. " If you want to know what your past thinking has been, look at your present circumstances. If you want to know what your future circumstances will be, look at your present thinking. Thanks for the great example of the frog soup, Animal."

He looked at the clock hanging on the wall above the empty platform and said, "Unfortunately, we are about out of time, so we'll just do a quick wrap-up of these four walls from today's session: 1. Fear of change, those thoughts that come up and scare us away from approaching the walls, 2. Apathy, just not caring after a while, 3. Inertia, the difficulty of getting started on something new or of changing a course we have been on for a while, and 4. Lack of a vision or of a larger purpose to our life. These obstacles apply to all of us, whether we are in here or outside. Remember, our thoughts create our lives. Next week we'll develop a couple tools that will help us climb out of our own mental prisons. See you next Friday."

CHAPTER EIGHT

The following Wednesday I sent a pass for Zeno to report to my office. He had received the pass by the time I passed through his gate that morning, so he asked me what it was about.

"Furlough," I answered.

"I never applied for furlough," he replied.

"I know. That is what I want to talk to you about."

The state of Ohio had just passed a law establishing the furlough program in Ohio prisons. It was designed to allow a man who had served a certain portion of his sentence, who had a good institutional record, a plan for employment and supervised living arrangements such as a halfway house to apply for an early release from the prison. It was more restrictive than parole, but obviously less restrictive than the prison itself. If an inmate was successfully managing his furlough, he would then most likely be granted parole status at his next parole hearing, which would allow him to move on to living at his home with his family and further normalizing his life.

It seemed to me that nearly every inmate at the Ohio Penitentiary thought himself to be a good candidate for furlough. My office was swamped with folded yellow messages called kites each morning from inmates wanting to apply. Some of the most dangerous men in Ohio applied, and I had to give a personal interview to each applicant, and then schedule them for a hearing before the furlough committee of which I was one of seven voting members. The first interview I conducted was with an inmate whose alias was "Crime Wave." Crime Wave was serving time for armed robbery and had several assaults on his record, including two assaults on other inmates. He was a compact, muscular man with a gold tooth and a tattoo of a tiger on

35

his shoulder. Ordinarily, I would not have known about the tattoo.

"What is your occupation," I asked as part of the interview.

"I'm an armed robber," he replied.

"I don't mean what is your crime, but what did you do for a living? Were you a carpenter, or an electrician, or something like that?"

"No, I'm an armed robber." He then went on to provide more information. "Do you know how to tell a professional armed robber from an amateur?" he asked.

"No, I don't," I replied.

He began to unbutton his shirt and I didn't know what was about to happen. He pulled the shirt off of his left shoulder, revealing a mark on top of his shoulder as well as the tattoo. "See that mark?" he asked with a measure of pride. "You get that mark from years of wearing a shoulder holster. That is how you tell a professional armed robber from someone who isn't serious about it." He then put his shirt back on and said, "Now, about my furlough application."

After spending weeks reviewing applications for furlough, I had sent a number of prospective furloughees' names to the committee for consideration. Yet I had not seen anyone that I thought was as good of a furlough candidate as Zeno – and he had not even applied. I had pulled his records and found that he had been convicted of first-degree murder and had served more than ten years on Death Row, then received a last minute stay of execution. When the U.S. Supreme Court shortly thereafter ruled that the death penalty was unconstitutional as it was then being applied, Zeno's sentence was commuted to life. He had served nearly 20 years, more than the minimum time for furlough consideration, and his institutional record was excellent for the past five and a half years. No write-ups, superb work reports, honor status, letters of commendation from the past three wardens, and from what I had personally seen, a strong desire to make a difference and help others. I was puzzled.

Zeno arrived promptly for his appointment. "Watch out for Crime Wave," he said as he sat down. "He's not too happy and he's blaming you for his not making furlough. I guess he's not familiar with the fourteenth passage from the *Enchiridion*," he added with a smile. The vote on Crime Wave's furlough had been 7-0 against, but I had cast the first vote and Crime Wave assumed that everyone just voted as I had. If I had voted yes, he thought everyone else would vote yes. I never understood why we voted in front of the inmates, but four of the others on the committee who did not work inside the walls thought openness was a great idea.

"Thanks for the heads up," I said. "But I want to talk with you about your furlough. I think with your record, you would stand an excellent chance of making it past the committee and have a fairly good chance with the parole board. Why haven't you applied?"

"I'm happy that you think I would be a good candidate, and I appreciate it that you are looking out for me. But furlough isn't in my plans right now."

"Why not?" I pressed him. I could see that he was searching for a way to answer the question, and it was a few moments before he replied.

"I don't know if I can explain it very well, or if it will make sense to you, but I have found a way to do time that works for me and provides me with both a sense of self-determination and an opportunity for atonement," he said. "I'm not ruling furlough out, but the time isn't right."

"If you don't mind my asking, I would be interested in knowing what you mean about how you do time."

"Remember the first words from the *Enchiridion*?" he asked.

"Yes, now I do. 'Some things are up to us and some things are not up to us.'"

"Well done," he laughed. "The idea behind that is to control what is up to you, but let the rest of it go. I initially thought that my being incarcerated was not up to me. Sure, I knew my crime was up to me and that being locked up was a natural consequence of the crime. But I did not see that my ongoing punishment was up to me, so I tried to just let it go. That helped me just go ahead and do the time, but it still left me with a feeling of irresponsibility and being controlled by others. I was reading a book by Thoreau when I came across a line that said 'When a dog charges you, call for him.' I wondered how I could use that in here. My prison sentence seemed like a dog charging me, but how could I call for it? I then realized that I could impose my own sentence on myself – kind of a concurrent sentence with the state sentence. I didn't disagree with my state sentence, and felt that I deserved to be here for a long time. So instead of having the state imposing a sentence on me, I mentally imposed it on myself. I concluded that I sentenced myself to prison the moment I committed my crime. I chose this, and I am still choosing it."

I was reminded of something called self-efficacy from a psychology class that I had taken at Ohio State. In the class the instructor had described an experiment done on undergraduate students in which students were divided into two groups. Each group had an electric wire attached to their finger through which electric current of increasing intensity could be run. One group had a switch with which they could turn off the current while the second group did not. The students were told to raise their hand when the discomfort became too great. The group with the switch was able to withstand much more discomfort than the group without the switch. The idea of being in control of the situation lowered their stress and enabled them to tolerate more discomfort. Now Zeno was showing me a practical application of this experiment in the laboratory of life. His taking responsibility for his actions and imposing a sentence on himself actually gave him a sense of self-direction and strength.

"How long is your sentence, then?"

"I didn't sentence myself to a set number of years – that is not up to me. I sentenced myself until I have atoned for my crime. I'm already remorseful, and always have been. But atoning is different. It cannot be imposed from outside or granted to someone just because he has served a number of years against his will. Epictetus taught that evil does not naturally dwell in the world or in people, but arises when we lose sight of our true aim in life, our true purpose. I know I can never undo my crime, but I believe that I still have a purpose on earth and by fulfilling it I will somehow get right with my life again. I'm not sure myself how that will happen, but I trust that I will know it *when* it happens. And when it happens, you just might find a kite on your desk from me."

Driving home that evening I thought about what Zeno said about taking responsibility for his incarceration, which was a step even beyond acceptance. I understood how Zeno's approach to his own situation was an empowerment that restored a sense of dignity and self-determination to him. It also allowed him the opportunity to somehow clean the slate of his past, or to atone, as he called it. Whatever good he would do in here would come from his own choices and not from being compelled by outside forces. That is part of the inner freedom that Epictetus valued so highly.

As I climbed into bed, I remembered something Zeno had said about Crime Wave: "I guess he's not familiar with the fourteenth passage from the *Enchiridion.*" I picked up my book from the nightstand, looked up the passage and read, "A person's master is someone who has power over what he craves or fears, either to obtain it or take it away. Whoever wants to be free, therefore, let him not crave or fear anything that is up to others. Otherwise he will necessarily be a slave."

CHAPTER NINE

Shakes was bursting with pride as the members filed into the group meeting. He was standing with Zeno looking at a new frame on the wall:

Round Two

A: It can't be done.

B: Is this true? Where does this thought lead? Is that where I want to go?

C: Think outside the box; see the problem from another angle.

It may have been the first time Shakes had ever been recognized for doing something positive, and he was relishing the moment. His thoughts were being displayed by Zeno for others to learn from. I then overheard him say to Zeno in an emotional voice, "I might die in prison, but I don't want to die a criminal. I have children out there, and this is hurting them big time. When you talked about the well and the box we live in last week, I thought that my body is imprisoned for the crime I committed, but if my thinking changes, grows outside the box, then I won't be a criminal any longer. My kids could honestly say that their dad is a good man. Do you think that is possible?"

"I'm sure of it, Shakes," Zeno replied.

At seven sharp the meeting began. Zeno again welcomed all of us and gave a quick review of our last meeting. "Who remembers what 'fail' means?" he asked.

Eddie spoke up. "Fear, Apathy, Inertia, Lack of Vision. These are the four walls that keep us in the box."

"Right. Tonight we're going to talk about getting past these walls – or to use Animal's terms, to leave the well and go to the ocean. And we'll start with a campfire by the water. I'm going to paint two scenarios for you and I would like for you to choose the one you would prefer. In the first scenario, you are walking by the campfire and you trip and fall and your hand goes into the fire. In the second scenario, you are walking by the campfire, you trip and fall, and your head hits a rock and knocks you out as your hand goes in the fire. Which of these two would you prefer?"

The men looked puzzled for a moment, then one of them said, "The first one."

"Why?" asked Zeno.

"Because I could pull my hand out right away." Some of the others nodded in agreement.

Another man said that he would prefer the second scenario "because I wouldn't feel the pain if I was knocked out." A few others shared his opinion.

The first man then said, "Just because you don't feel the pain doesn't mean that damage isn't being done. What will happen to your hand if you don't pull it out of the fire?"

The second man then admitted that it would probably burn off, and he asked if he could change his answer to the first scenario.

"Pain and consequences have a good purpose," explained Zeno, "but only if we pay attention to them. They can motivate us to make changes, to pull our hand out of the fire, but only if we are aware of them. Consequences without awareness are ineffective." By now everyone was agreeing that the first scenario would be the better choice – that it would be better to feel the pain for a moment to avoid long term damage.

"All of us in here have probably had our hand in the fire for some time, but we have ways of playing it off, making it seem like no big deal," he said as he pulled his right hand up into his sleeve to the laughs of the men. "How do we keep ourselves unconscious to the negative consequences and pain we have brought into our lives?"

"By doing drugs and alcohol," answered Shakes. "That is what I did, and I woke up in here – with a ten year headache!"

"Hanging out with my friends who are into the same stuff as me – they all have just one hand, too, so it looks normal to us," offered another.

"I hang out with people who have no hands – that way I look really good while I'm burning up," added a third man.

"Just telling myself it's not so bad, even though it is," said another.

"Not thinking about it at all."

"Being the life of the party is how I did it," said Animal.

"You guys get the idea," said Zeno. "We have ways to block out the pain and consequences in our lives, and to even make ourselves look good while we do it, but we still get the negative results, no matter what. Since we all agreed that it is better to pull our hand out of the fire as soon as possible, let's do a little activity to increase our awareness of the consequences. This is not to show us how bad we are, but to show us how bad of a life we are creating and to motivate us to make changes – to save ourselves and our families from further damage."

He then introduced the next activity by quoting Epictetus: "Determine what happens first, consider what that leads to, and then act in accordance with what you've learned." Zeno asked the men to consider some of the results they had received from living a criminal lifestyle, and they went around the circle taking turns as Zeno listed their answers on the board. Loss of freedom, stress, anger, debts, loss of respect from family, loss of self-respect, bad role model for their kids, loss of job, depression, health problems, anxiety and looking over your shoulder all the time were the first round answers. The board filled up after a couple more rounds of answers, and Zeno then broke the list into categories: physical, emotional, social, mental, financial, spiritual, and he added one more category – others. "Who else pays these prices right along with us?" he asked.

"My kids," answered Shakes immediately.

"My employer lost a lot behind this," said Leonard. "By the time he found and trained someone to take my place, he almost went under. And that would have cost his other workers their jobs, too."

"The taxpayers also lose," said Animal.

"I don't agree with that," said another. "I've been paying taxes all my life, so this is just getting my own money back."

"Are you saying that instead of *your* taxes going to roads, schools, and hospitals, they were going for your future stay in prison?" replied Animal. "Instead of an Individual Retirement Account, you set up an Individual Incarceration Account? I can just see the banker's face on that one!"

The group cracked up, with the first man finally agreeing that the taxpayers did, in fact, pay for his room and board at the Walls. Some of the other answers Zeno listed on the board included victims and their families, parents, aunts, uncles, nieces and nephews, society, and friends.

"Now please take out a piece of paper and draw a circle in the middle of it about the size of a quarter. In the circle write the words 'old life'. This represents the old life that you were living that led to your coming to prison. Draw four short stems off of that circle and put a circle at the end of each of those stems. In each of these four circles write one price that you are paying or have paid for that life. Think of a price from several of the categories, but one of your circles must include the word 'others.'"

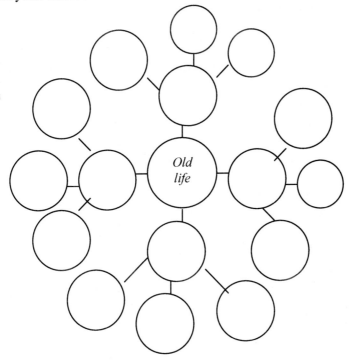

After a couple minutes the men had completed filling in the circles. Zeno then instructed them to draw three stems off each of the four circles and write in a price in each circle that was the result of the earlier circle. "For example, if you listed stress in one of your circles, ask yourself 'what does this lead to?' Maybe it leads to anger, which you would put in one of the three circles off of ⤶ stress. Maybe it causes fights with your wife or girlfriend. Or maybe when you're stressed you get headaches. With each circle ask yourself, 'what does this lead to?' and then write it in a circle. Off of the 'others' circle draw three circles and put the names of three people who are paying these prices along with you, and then from those circles follow it out with how they are paying and what that leads to for them."

After another minute or so Zeno said, "I'm going to give you some time to keep doing this. Keep drawing new stems and circles off of each previous circle and put in a price that is caused by the preceding circle. And while it may not seem like it, the more circles you can come up with, the better."

The men were completely absorbed in the task until Zeno eventually stopped them and asked them to look at their diagrams and make any observations they could about the circles.

"I can't believe how much trouble can come from just one thing!"

"It's all negative."

"I keep seeing the same things popping up in more than one circle."

"How many of you noticed the same old thing repeating itself?" asked Zeno.

All hands went up. "It's like a dog chasing its tail around in a circle," noted Eddie. "All mine eventually lead to anger, jail, drugs, or death, no matter which of the four circles I started with."

"I never realized how many other people were hurt by my actions. I just never thought about it before, and I can't believe what I see here – but I have to believe it, cause it's right here in front of me!" said another. "Selling drugs leads to getting arrested that leads to being away from my kids that leads to them having problems in school that leads to my oldest boy quitting school that leads to him having a lot of problems with employment and finances. It's almost overwhelming for me to see this. This can affect my future grandkids - and I thought I was doing something to help my family!"

Everyone sat quietly for a few minutes looking at the results of their old life on the papers they held in their hands.

Another group member who had not spoken at the previous meeting finally broke the silence. "Our traditions teach that one should consider the effects of his actions on the next seven generations," offered Manny, a Native American about thirty years old with coal black hair and deep-set eyes. He was studying the traditional teachings of his people and was challenging the rule in court that all inmates must wear short hair. "If you can say that your actions will not harm your descendants, then you may go ahead and act."

"That is certainly taking a long view outside the box, Manny," said Zeno. "Thank you for sharing the ancient wisdom from your culture. It's interesting to see how similar some of these old teachings are. If I may go back to our campfire example for a minute, by doing the circle exercise we are now more likely to pull our hands out of the fire before we burn them off because we are now conscious of the pain. What you have done here is not give yourself any more negative consequences than you had before – you just increased your awareness of the prices you and others are already paying or will likely pay in the future. And who knows - it may very well affect the next seven generations, like Manny said."

Zeno drew the nine dots on the board, and then placed just one circle in the nine dots. "Not thinking about what leads to what keeps us in the box." He then drew the stems and circles off of the first circle so they fell outside the box, and said, "All of these prices you identified beyond the first circle represent an increased awareness, or thinking outside the box. And thinking outside the box leads to a life outside the box.

"This circle exercise is a mental tool that we can use to move beyond the F.A.I.L. barriers that keep us in the box. The first of these barriers is fear. When you think about actually changing, what are some fears that come up?"

"I'm afraid that I would lose my friends if I changed my ways," said one man.

"I'm afraid I'd have a boring life."

"I'd miss the fast and easy money," said another to the nods of several group members.

"I'm afraid I'd fail and just fall back into my old ways."

"I'm afraid of the temptations."

"I'd lose the respect of my associates if I changed."

Zeno listed these fears on the board, and then asked each man to write his fear on a piece of paper. "Now hold your paper with the fear on it at arm's length in your left hand and your circle page at arm's length in your right hand. That is the trade you are making – you are paying all of those prices in your right hand to not face the fear in your left hand."

He then turned to the man who feared losing his friends and asked him if his friends were worth all the prices in his circles, which included being alone in the prison and away from his friends. "I can see that my old ways actually caused the very thing I said I feared – I'm more alone now than ever. Plus, there is no way any friends are worth all the prices I'm paying. Hell, I never hear from them anyway now that I'm locked up."

Zeno then asked another man if he enjoyed the repetitive routines and day-to-day sameness of getting up at the same time, marching to the mess hall at the same time, getting counted at the same time, going to the commissary at the same time, and going to bed at the same time.

"Hell, no, you'd have to be crazy to like that!" he answered.

"But that is exactly what you are getting in your effort to not be bored, isn't it?"

"I see what you mean – I'm paying the price of living a boring life so that I don't have to risk living a boring life. It's the dog chasing his tail again, isn't it."

"Before you say anything else, Zeno, I already see what fast and easy money has brought me," said Eddie. "When I look at all the circles in my right hand, that fast and easy money was anything *but* fast and easy. I would have done much better with a minimum wage job if you count all the time and money it has cost me – not to mention what it has done to my family."

"And my fear of failing brings me circles such as stress, depression, anger, loss of family, debts, lost jobs,

49

and so much more. I can hardly say that all these circles represent a resounding success!" confessed another man.

Zeno then addressed the idea of temptation. "What is it that makes something tempting to us?" asked Zeno.

"Obviously it is something that we want and like," answered the man who had listed a fear of temptations.

"Right. But if you look at the big picture and see where it all leads, you may find it is not as tempting. If you include being locked up, away from your family, and all the other circles on your paper, you'll find that those old temptations are suddenly not as tempting as before. Think big picture, outside the box."

At this point, Animal chimed in, saying that reminded him of a dog story. "If you don't count all of the long term prices in these circles," he said, "it is like trying to just walk the front half of a dog. We all like the front half of the dog – it licks you, you get to feed it, and all that – but we don't want what comes out the back half of the dog – the smelly messy part. But a dog has both ends, and so do our actions. You can't just take the front half of the dog for a walk – like partying or doing crimes – without taking the back half. You have to take the whole dog."

"And a pooper-scooper," added Eddie to the laughter of the others.

"Thanks, Animal – I guess!" said Zeno good-naturedly. He then moved on to the man who listed losing the respect of other inmates. Zeno pointed out that Epictetus saw this as a particularly harmful fear, and quoted from the *Enchiridion*: "Those who pursue a better life must be prepared to be ridiculed or criticized by their former associates. Many people who have progressively lowered their personal standards in order to win acceptance from others will bitterly resent those who seek to better themselves. Never live your life in reaction to those poor souls. Be compassionate toward them, and at the same time hold to what you know is good. It is your job to carry yourself with quiet dignity and to stick to your ideals and goals. Cling to what you know in your heart is best. If you are steadfast, those very ones who ridiculed you will come to admire you.'"

After the discussion of how to counter fears with the circle diagram, which he compared to a warrior's shield that can protect us from bad decisions, Zeno moved on to the other walls of the box. "You can also use these circles to counter the next two letters in F.A.I.L. – apathy and inertia," he said. "Motivation is the great counterpunch to fear, apathy and inertia, and if all these prices we are paying don't motivate us to care and make an effort to change, I don't know what will. Epictetus said that a half-hearted spirit has no power and that tentative efforts lead to tentative outcomes. Use these circles to power up your motivation to move out of the well.

"There is one letter left in our four letters of F.A.I.L., and Epictetus thought it is the most important one – lack of vision or purpose. In fact, he said that evil did not exist naturally in the world or in people, but was a byproduct of forgetting our true aim and purpose in life. We are out of time tonight, but next week we'll talk about that one. Have a good week, gentlemen." And with that the men walked out of the Death House and across the cold, windswept yard to their cells.

CHAPTER TEN

The new frame on the wall the following week summed up one of the chief observations from the previous week's session:

Round Three

A: If I ignore the prices, I won't have to pay them.

B: Is this true? Where does this thought lead? Is that where I want to go?

C: If I ignore the prices, I'll pay even more in the long run!

To start the meeting, Zeno shared a story to illustrate the importance of being focused on our purpose, our true aim. "Once in ancient India there was a tournament held to test marksmanship in archery. A wooden fish was set up on a high pole and the eye of the fish was the target. One by one many valiant princes came and tried their skill, but in vain. Before each one shot his arrow the teacher asked him what he saw, and invariably all replied that they saw a fish on a pole at a great height with head, eyes, clouds in the sky or trees behind it, and so on; but the final archer, as he took his aim, said 'I see the eye of the fish,' and he was the only one who succeeded in hitting the mark." As Zeno finished the story he gave me a look and a smile that let me know that he knew about my experience of the preceding day – but how did he find out about that?

"That story comes from India," said Zeno, "but Epictetus also taught that it was purpose that gave our life meaning, strengthened our will and gave our life coherence. He taught that if we were lazy, forgetful, or distracted and took our eye off of the target, our lives would come to misery and pain. He believed that purpose came from God, which in his day was represented by Zeus or other gods. The philosophers of Epictetus's time were the moral leaders and teachers and instructed the people in how to live a good life, while the religious leaders of the day were concerned primarily with performing rituals. His devotion can be found in the Prayer of Epictetus: 'Lead me, Zeus and Destiny, whithersoever I am appointed to go. I will follow without wavering; even though I turn coward and shrink, I shall follow all the same.'

"He saw himself as a teacher and felt that was his nature and purpose. He taught that one should be totally concerned with his own purpose, what he called his nature, and not be distracted by things that fall outside of one's purpose or nature. He said that that is how one can live a life of peace and tranquility."

"The Prayer of Epictetus reminds me of one of the sacred traditions of our people," said Manny. "It is called a Vision Quest, and is a prayer to Manitou, or Great Spirit, to show us what our purpose is, our path through this life. I feel that my problems have come from not following my path, or what Epictetus calls purpose. I was raised on the rez and attended what they called an Indian school. It was a government school, and was anything *but* an Indian school. We were told not to speak our own language, or observe our own customs and spiritual practices. As a result, I was not being true to my own nature, and became lost like so many of my brothers and sisters. After leaving the reservation, I finally got into big enough trouble that I came to prison, and while I was here I started studying the traditional ways of my people. One of those practices was the vision quest. This was how a young man found his purpose – he went out into the desert or on a mountain for three or four days, sat inside a circle of stones, and prayed for a vision. When he received it, he came back to the tribe and shared it with a wise elder who interpreted it for him. It seems to me that one of the keys to the vision quest is removing yourself from your ordinary day-to-day life. Being away from familiar things and the people who know you helps you see in a new way, with new eyes. That newness and openness allows for the new vision to happen. One day I realized that my time in this penitentiary, surrounded by these walls of stone, could be my own personal vision quest – I am away from familiar things and people and have time to pray and look at myself and my life with new eyes. This prison can be whatever you make it – and I'm making it a vision quest for myself. That is one of the reasons I come to this group."

"I can't see any purpose that somebody can have locked up in this godforsaken place," said Leonard. "To the people on the other side of these walls driving down Neil Avenue, we don't even exist."

For the first time since I had been coming to the meetings, Zeno revealed something about himself during the session. "It doesn't matter if anyone knows you exist, you know it and God knows it. I understand what Manny is saying about using this place as a vision quest – because that is what I have done, although I didn't call it that. I found out that I belong right here – and not only because I committed a crime. I believe I have been placed here to serve a very important purpose for society, whether they know it or not or whether they appreciate it or not. I don't see myself as being outside of society, I see myself at the turning point of a lot of lives. Almost every man in here will one day be released back into society, and if he finds something that can help him lead a good and decent life as a result of coming to our meetings, then I have made a positive contribution. Epictetus taught that living in accordance with one's nature is the root of happiness, and I have found that to be true. It isn't money, or fame, that does it – and I had both when I was boxing. It is about your character and living in harmony with that. In the end, that is all any of us have, it's all we take with us. If character is wealth, I have as much of an opportunity to die a rich man as anyone on the outs."

"I believe you are happy, Zeno," said Eddie. "If living your purpose does it, I want some of that for myself. But how do I find it?"

"There is no simple formula, but there are some ways to approach the problem. Like Manny said, for some people it involves prayer and meditation, but for others it may require action. It can be simply doing the right thing, time after time, meeting the demands of each day with courage and resoluteness. The writer Ralph Waldo Emerson said that the talent is the call. What are you good at? You may need to try many things to find your skill or talent. A professor named Joseph Campbell said that we are all on a hero's journey if only we would answer the call – but most people don't, they stay safe in their old routines and comfort zones – in their own wells. The call for him was what makes you happy. He said 'Follow your bliss.' Another kind of purpose is compassion, or love. But love is not the mushy sentiment you hear so often in here, it is not just a feeling, it is made up of actions. Being supportive of your kids, writing letters as much as you can to them, even staying out of trouble in here so you get home as soon as possible can be your purpose."

Shakes then spoke up, asking if something like just being a good father could be someone's purpose.

"Watch out for the word 'just'," answered Zeno. "It is a way to minimize the importance of something. Being a good father might be your highest purpose, and when you lost track of that, you ended up doing things that got you in trouble. One's purpose does not have to be big and showy – the simplest things can have the greatest effects."

"Then I know what I'm going to do. My goal is to earn a good conduct visit with my kids."

The rules at the Ohio Penitentiary allowed for only one visit per month from each person on the inmate's approved visiting list. If an inmate were able to maintain a clear conduct record for six months, he would earn a good conduct visit – an extra visit from someone on his list. Any rule infraction that resulted in a visit to the correctional cell caused the six-month clock to be reset to zero. Offenses could range from agitating, gambling, and fighting to insolence, mushfaking, or being out of place (not being where he is supposed to be). In the sea of provocation that was the Ohio Pen, a six-month clear conduct record was indeed an achievement worthy of the extra visit, and could represent a significant "gift" from an inmate to a family that wanted to see him. Shakes had never earned one – in fact, he had never come close.

"That sounds like a good purpose to me," said Zeno. "Remember the eye of the fish – the good conduct visit – and not get caught up or distracted by other things if you want to achieve it. Use the ABC Model of Inner Boxing when thoughts come up that would take you off target."

Zeno then offered a word of caution about finding your purpose. "Epictetus taught that 'the natural instinct of man is self-preservation and self-interest, yet men are so constituted that the individual cannot secure his own interest unless he contributes to the common welfare.' That means that purely selfish desires and actions do not constitute one's purpose, so you must consider the effects on others when you seek your purpose."

We then did a variation on last week's circle exercise to confront the L in the F.A.I.L. model – a lack of vision or purpose. "If you will recall from our nine dots diagram, a lack of vision is one of the four walls that keeps us confined in the box. Tonight we will start to develop a vision for ourselves, a target to begin focusing on, and a life that can draw us out of our well – like Shakes' vision of earning the extra visit and being a good father."

We began the exercise by drawing a circle in the middle of a piece of paper, like last week, but this time we wrote the word "change" in the circle. "Let the word change represent the new life you want to create for yourself."

"Could it be going to Marion instead of Lucasville?" asked one man. Marion was a medium-security prison, while Lucasville was the new maximum-security prison. Busses were pulling out almost daily for both destinations.

"It could be, but the problem with that is that it is up to the Classification Committee to make that decision. If you focus on your part of that, which is keeping a clean record here, it could work."

After the men had written "change" in the first circle, they were instructed to draw four stems and circles off of that circle and to think of the emotional, social, mental, physical, financial, and other benefits that could come from that circle. "You might want to put a goal in some of the circles, like taking a class in auto repair or getting your GED, or it may be something like working to become less angry, or maybe helping others," he suggested. Like last week, we were to write the word "others" in one of the first four circles, and to think of the benefits that these other people would gain along with us. We were given several minutes to keep drawing stems and circles off of each circle, asking ourselves "What benefit or positive result could come from that circle?"

The atmosphere in the room was much lighter this week as the men began developing a positive vision of what their life could become. You could sense hopefulness and relief as one circle after another was filled in. After about ten minutes, Zeno stopped us and listed on the board some of the things that the men had included in their circles. Inner peace, better family relationships, trust, good health, good job, education, kids having a better life, financial stability, freedom, less anger, more tolerance, and being at home were just some of the benefits listed. He then asked us to look at our papers and share any observations we might make.

"This felt a whole lot better," offered one man immediately to the head shakes of the others.

"I was surprised that this felt easier to me," said another. "It had more of a flow to it."

"I have no experience with anything positive like this, so it was harder for me to think of things to put in my circles at first" said another. "But when I could start thinking of some things, I saw that they would lead to a better life."

"I was amazed at how many others would benefit from it as well as me."

"This week it felt like things were opening up, blossoming out. Last week it felt like things were narrowing down, like I was just squeezing myself into a smaller and smaller life. I guess the old life circles create a smaller and smaller well, but the change circles take us out of the well and to the ocean, like Animal said."

"This is a good first step toward living a life of purpose, a life we can be proud of, a life that helps others as well as ourselves," Zeno pointed out. "We replace the *f*ear, *a*pathy, *i*nertia, and *l*ack of vision that spell out F.A.I.L. with *h*ope, *o*pportunity, *p*ossibility, and *e*nthusiasm that spell H.O.P.E.

"Having a vision of what is possible allows us to see opportunities when they arise. If you have no goal or purpose, when something comes up you won't see how it can be of benefit to you and others. With a positive vision in your mind, you will see opportunities arise and have more enthusiasm to pursue them. You will find that you may become suddenly 'luckier', but all it is is seeing things that help you reach your goal and vision.

"You may also find that you are not alone as you work toward your purpose. I have learned to just trust the process. You still have to work at it, but I also believe that we get help from some other source – call it God, Zeus, Higher Self, Coincidence, or Stanley, it doesn't matter, but it is there. For me, it started with finding the Epictetus book under the mattress in my new cell, then the group formed itself with interested people wanting to share and learn together, and recently when we lost the chaplain as our advisor, Mr. Traylor arrived here and volunteered to take over without even being asked.

"There is a quotation I came across from a man named Goethe," Zeno said. He then pulled out a book and read aloud, "'until one is committed, there is hesitancy, the chance to draw back, always ineffectiveness.... The moment one definitely commits oneself, then Providence moves, too. All sorts of things occur to help one that would never otherwise have occurred... boldness has genius, power and magic in it. Begin it now.'"

With those words, the evening's session came to a close. After I had signed all the passes and the men had gone, I stopped to talk with Zeno for a moment.

"That was a very interesting session tonight. I especially liked that archery story, but I have one question, Zeno. From the look and smile you gave me when you told the story, I know you knew about my shooting incident yesterday. How did you find out?"

"I had to run an errand for the deputy warden over to C block, and the guards in the block were really razzing Bull pretty heavy. Saying things like 'I hear a social worker out shot you yesterday' and 'The furlough counselor is taking your place on the riot squad' and things like that. I figured you must have done some impressive shooting on the range."

"Not some shooting – I only got to fire one shot," I said. "My prowess is being exaggerated."

All employees were required to take weapons training, and I had been told to report to the range. I was the only social worker-type there, and was lined up with about a half dozen corrections officers. Social workers are not generally noted for their marksmanship, and to make matters worse, I had never even fired a gun. The instructor had each of us line up in a row in front of paper targets with the silhouette of a man on them. He then told us to load our pistols. I had to stop him at that point, and with all the others watching, ask him how to load my gun. That drew hearty laughter and snickers from my fellow marksmen, especially the man on my right called Bull. After I finally succeeded in getting the bullets into my gun, the instructor resumed his instructions.

"Here is the situation," he said. "We are in a riot situation, and an inmate is approaching you in the hall. He has his right hand in his pocket and you have ordered him to remove it from his pocket and keep it in plain sight. He has not complied. Begin firing and continue firing at the target until you hit it in the area of the right wrist."

The line erupted in gunfire as the officers commenced shooting at their targets. As for me, my first shot went precisely through the target's right wrist. Bull, who was banging away on my right, looked at me with disbelief. I blew the smoke away from the barrel of my gun and slid it back into its holster. I then stood watching and waiting for him to hit his target, which I'm sure only caused him more trouble, as he was missing by bigger and bigger margins. He finally ran out of ammunition.

"Nice try, don't give up, ask for some more bullets," I encouraged him, but he seemed unappreciative. Just then it began thundering and we had to abandon the range, bringing to an end my weapons training – and the beginning of my legend as the gunslinging social worker.

"So, as you can see, Zeno, it was just beginner's luck," I said.

"Or beginner's mind," he answered. "Beginner's luck assumes there is no rational explanation for it – but there is. You had an open mind when it came to shooting

61

skills– you had no preconceived ideas, you had developed no bad habits, you kept it simple and uncluttered. You could see clearly, without the haze of prejudices or habits or experience. Although you and Bull didn't know it, you had an unfair advantage over him!"

I had never thought of experience as being a disadvantage before, but Zeno went on to offer an unusual view on the subject.

"When we come into the world, we are what you could call 'bright' – we are inquisitive and curious, open to learning and seeing the world with new eyes. As we gain experience, we may develop notions that the way we have always done something is the only way, the 'right' way, to do it. We then wall ourselves off to other ideas and opinions – we keep ourselves *in* the box by keeping new information and possibilities *out*. We can think of this second stage as being 'too bright.' The 'too bright' stage is stifling – in the joint, we say someone in this stage might be institutionalized. In fact, even institutions get institutionalized!" he laughed. "If an individual is smart, they move to the next stage – where they are again open to new possibilities and ideas, using their experience as a positive resource but not as a wall to keep other ideas out. In this more advanced stage we have let go of our preconceived ideas and rigid thinking habits that we had in the 'too bright' stage, we are flexible and innovative, and life gets fresh and new again, ripe with possibility and optimism. I call this third stage the '*not* too bright' stage. So now when someone says to me, 'Zeno, you're not too bright,' I say 'thank you very much – I work hard to stay that way!'"

I laughed while admiring Zeno's ability to stand "common sense" on its head, to take a new view of things, and to see things from outside the box.

As I took my leave of Zeno, he called out, "Eye of the fish."

"Eye of the fish," I called back, and walked out of the institution.

My drive home that night had me thinking not just about beginner's mind but also about my own purpose in life. What was it? Could I be living it now? I had not planned on a career in corrections any more than Zeno had planned the creation of the Epictetus Club – yet he still saw it as his purpose. Could your purpose choose you as much as you chose your purpose? I had not applied for the job at the pen, but had been called as a result of a state civil service test I had taken months earlier for social worker jobs. My only intent in taking the prison interview was to see inside the castle-like fortress that I had been seeing from the outside since childhood. I already had my bags packed, literally, to return to Berkeley, California where I had spent half of my 18 months since graduating from Ohio State.

During the interview, I was told that the job I was interviewing for would only last six months, since the prison was in the process of shutting down. There was no guarantee of anything after that. That actually made the job more attractive to me, since I could get some experience to put on my resume without committing to a long stint. I accepted the offer and went home and unpacked my bags. I had become an official employee of the Ohio Penitentiary – until March, anyway – and would soon become the advisor of a club named for an ancient Greek I had never heard of. Could Zeus be at work here?

CHAPTER ELEVEN

It was late by the time I got home from the meeting, so I grabbed a snack and went to bed. The telephone jarred me awake at 3:00 A.M.

"Mr. Traylor?" asked the voice. "This is Associate Warden Cochran at the penitentiary."

I knew this couldn't be good – especially since it was Mr. Cochran calling. Prisons are generally split into two divisions, one custody and the other treatment. The two factions are usually at odds, with the custody staff thinking the treatment staff coddles criminals, and the treatment staff thinking the custody staff is insensitive and simply punitive. Cochran was the head of custody and not in my chain of command – except in emergencies.

"We've had an apparent escape this evening. Inmate Hickerson was missing at the midnight count and we have been unable to locate him after a sweep of the institution. We wanted you to know, since we have heard that he was upset after his furlough hearing."

Hickerson. Hickerson. I racked my sleepy brain to place the name. Then it hit me – Hickerson was Crime Wave's real name.

"Do you own a gun?" asked Mr. Cochran.

I didn't, but my housemate Andy had a pistol stashed somewhere in the house that he used for target practice at his cabin in Pennsylvania.

"I can get access to one right away," I answered.

"I would suggest that you do it. I don't want to alarm you, but it is better to be prepared just in case. He may very well be on his way out of state by now, and the last thing he would want to do is delay his getaway with a visit to you – but you never know."

"Thanks for calling me," I said as I hung up the phone. I then woke up Andy and told him what had happened. We got his pistol, loaded it and put it in the towel closet in the hallway between our rooms. If Crime Wave was coming for me, Andy was at just as much risk as I was. After a sleepless night, we decided to commune with nature at the cabin in Pennsylvania for the rest of the weekend. We grabbed a few clothes, the pistol, and my copy of the *Enchiridion* and jumped into our cars – Andy decided to stay for the next week since he was off for a few days, but I had to be back for work on Monday.

The hills of Pennsylvania where Andy's cabin was located was remote and beautiful. We spent some time target shooting, but I wasn't sure if that made me more comfortable or more nervous. After night fell, I decided to see if Epictetus had anything to say on the topic, so I picked up the *Enchiridion* and began reading.

It only took a few minutes to find my answers to both my questions about purpose and a way to deal with the fear and anxiety I was having as a result of Crime Wave's escape. In the 17th passage in the handbook I read, "Remember that you are an actor in a play, which is as the playwright wants it to be: short if he wants it short, long if he wants it long. If he wants you to play a beggar, play even this part skillfully, or a cripple, or a public official, or a private citizen. What is yours is to play the assigned part well. But to choose it belongs to someone else."

As I was reflecting on the circumstances of my getting my job, I remembered Mr. Burkhart telling me if I had correction fluid in my veins instead of blood, this would be my life's work. I knew I liked the work, and enjoyed working with the inmates, especially the ones in the Epictetus Club. My enjoyment of the job (present circumstance notwithstanding) meant I was "following my bliss." If the "talent was the call," I felt that I was off to a good start at what I was doing, and could become better. And the fact that I was in the position without choosing it was perhaps Zeus at work, putting me where I was supposed to be.

A calm came over me as I realized that everything in my life had constellated to create my present circumstance, and rather than resist it out of fear of Crime Wave, I could embrace it with courage, faith and trust. I silently said the Prayer of Epictetus that Zeno had recited at the last meeting: 'Lead me, Zeus and Destiny, whithersoever I am appointed to go. I will follow without wavering; even though I turn coward and shrink, I shall follow all the same.' This is what I was supposed to be doing, it was my part in the play. It was not up to me if it was a short play or a long play, my part was only to play it well. I remembered Epictetus saying to the emperor who wanted his head, "My purpose is to teach. If your purpose is to take off my head, then go ahead. You do what you have to do, and I'll do what I have to do." My decision about Crime Wave's furlough was the right one, and I would make it again. If Crime Wave wanted my head, so be it. The next morning I packed up and headed home.

Driving in to work Monday morning I caught the news on the radio. "Ronald Hickerson, the Ohio Penitentiary inmate who escaped early Saturday morning, was shot and killed by a motorist when he forced his way into the man's automobile and told the man to drive away. The driver, an off-duty security guard, pulled a gun from under his seat and shot the escapee in the head. Hickerson, who had served a little more than two years of a 10 – 25 year sentence for armed robbery from Cuyahoga County, was pronounced dead at the scene. Warden Cartwright said that an investigation is underway to determine how Hickerson escaped. In other news..."

CHAPTER TWELVE

The prison had been abuzz for days about the escape. Rumors abounded on the grapevine about how Crime Wave had gotten out. One story had him tunneling under the wall, another had him carving a hole through the wall, and another had him climbing over the wall. The most likely method was that he had managed to hide himself in a garbage truck that left the prison earlier that evening, avoiding a search by stashing himself in the garbage bin of the truck. However he did it, the prison would probably be closed by the time the answers would be found. Anyway, it was old news by the time the next Epictetus Club meeting rolled around. Zeno had stayed focused that week and had hung a new frame on the wall that I especially liked:

> # Round Four
>
> ## *The Prayer of Epictetus*
>
> *Lead me, Zeus and Destiny,*
> *whithersoever I am appointed*
> *to go. I will follow without*
> *wavering; even though I turn*
> *coward and shrink, I shall*
> *follow all the same.*

The meeting came to order promptly at seven, with Zeno welcoming the members and then moving on to the night's topic. "A half-hearted spirit has no power, according to Epictetus. And power is a very important part of change. We can have good intentions, but without any power to carry out our plans we will not succeed. Mike, what is the main way that your stock car might lose serious power?" asked Zeno of one of the men.

Mike, an experienced stock car driver and mechanic, answered that one of the ways was by having a blown head gasket. "You can have all the horses in the world under your hood, but if you don't have the compression, you don't have the muscle. Some of your power is blowing out through the hole in the gasket instead of being directed toward powering your car toward the finish line."

"There are some things we do with our thinking that also cause us to lose power, or to lose compression," said Zeno. "And if we do these things, even though we have good motivation and a good target, we still won't make it to our finish line or to our goal. Tonight we're going to do a sort of compression check – to see if we've blown a head gasket ourselves."

"I know I've blown a gasket or two in my time," said Leonard. Most of the others agreed.

"Sometimes it's obvious when we've blown a gasket – like when we're enraged and flying off the handle. But there are other times when it is so subtle we might not even realize that it has happened."

He then asked the men to think of the reasons they used to justify their crimes as he wrote their answers on the board.

"I was drunk," volunteered the first man.

"I needed the money."

"I was snitched on."

"My parole officer was out to get me."

"I didn't do it," another man said to the laughter of the others.

"The guy driving got pulled over and they found the drugs on me. If he hadn't run that stop sign I wouldn't be here."

"My kid needed diapers."

"I didn't have a job."

"I don't have a good enough education to get a job, so I had to do what I did."

"My old lady pissed me off."

"I grew up in the projects."

"I was high on drugs."

"I didn't think I'd get caught," said the last man in the circle.

Zeno then read a passage from the *Enchiridion*: "Blaming others is silly. When we suffer setbacks, disturbances or grief, let us never place the blame on others, but on our own attitudes. Small-minded people habitually blame others for their misfortunes. Average people blame themselves. Those who are dedicated to a life of self-mastery understand that the impulse to blame something or someone is foolishness, that there is nothing to be gained in blaming, whether it be others or oneself. Blaming oneself puts you down and is not the same as taking responsibility. Taking responsibility empowers a person, giving them a chance to learn from their mistakes and make changes. *One of the signs of the dawning of self-mastery is the gradual elimination of blame.*"

Zeno then added, "Simply making excuses is a way to blow a gasket and lose our power to change. We end up feeling helpless, blaming others, and giving our power away to whoever or whatever we are blaming." He then pointed to the list on the board and asked, "What do you notice when you look at this list?"

"We might think of them as reasons, but they are really a lot of excuses!" said Eddie.

"Eddie's right – the list is a load of B.S.," agreed Leonard.

"One of the best ways to get power back over our own lives, to repair that blown head gasket, is to see our excuses for what they are," said Zeno. "Simply identifying them is a great step forward. To use our ABC Model of Inner Boxing, these excuses are like the attacking thoughts we are using against ourselves. We can block them by being aware that they are excuses and are robbing us of our own power. Let's see if we can come up with some counterpunches to each of these thoughts. Let's do some work on the speed bag – how fast can you counter your own attacking thought with a productive thought that restores your power? Repeat the attacking thought and then counter it."

Shakes went first. "Attacking thought: I was drunk; counterpunch: I drank and got myself drunk."

"Good job," encouraged Zeno. "Next."

"Attacking thought: I needed the money; counterpunch: everyone needs money. I could get a job or borrow it or find some other way to get money besides crime."

"Attacking thought: I was snitched on; counterpunch: if I hadn't set myself up by doing the crime the snitch wouldn't have had anything to use on me."

"You guys are doing great. Next," said Zeno.

"Attacking thought: My parole officer was out to get me; counterpunch: what the hell am I doing with a parole officer anyway!"

"Attacking thought: I didn't do it; counterpunch: okay, I did it."

"Attacking thought: The guy driving got pulled over; counterpunch: if I didn't have drugs on me, he would have just got a ticket and I wouldn't have gotten anything. As it is, he lost his car and I went to prison."

"Attacking thought: my kid needed diapers; counterpunch: there are better ways to get diapers."

"Attacking thought: I didn't have a job; counterpunch: go look for a job!"

"Attacking thought: I don't have a good education; counterpunch: go to school and get an education."

"Attacking thought: my old lady pissed me off; counterpunch: I pissed myself off, and being pissed is no excuse to hit anyone."

"Attacking thought: I grew up in the projects; counterpunch: so, I grew up in the projects. Not everybody in the projects goes to jail."

"Attacking thought: I was high on drugs; counterpunch: I got high to get rid of my fear so I could do the crime. The fact is, I was doing crimes before I ever did drugs."

"That is a powerful insight. Nice counterpunch!" Zeno responded. "Next."

"Attacking thought: I won't get caught; counterpunch, I will get caught!"

"Great job, guys," said Zeno. "How did that feel?"

"Strangely enough, it felt better than the excuses I've been using. All along I thought that if I admitted the truth I would feel worse, but I actually feel stronger and more hopeful. I can't change the things I was blaming, but I can change myself. The attacking thought seemed beyond my control, but the counterpunch is something I can do, something that is up to me," replied Leonard.

"When I saw those so-called reasons on the board, I was kind of embarrassed because I saw through them right away, so I know that others see through mine too. Just because they don't call me on it doesn't mean they don't see it. And here I thought I was making myself look good!" added another group member.

"It actually seems easier to step up to the plate and own up now. I wear myself out trying to keep my stories straight and remembering what I said to who."

"I confess that I actually started believing my own stuff after a while, since I said it so often. I must look like a fool to the people I was lying to. No wonder no one believes me even when I tell the truth – its like the boy who cried wolf so many times no one came to help him when the wolf really showed up."

"I see that I made up my excuse to keep from feeling guilty and ashamed. And when I see my counterpunch, I do feel guilty for what I've done."

"Guilt can be a healthy emotion," answered Zeno. "It can motivate us to change and to live a better life. But if we keep trying to avoid it, it can't do its job. Healthy guilt is guilt that prompts us to make a positive change. After it's done that and you've made the change, let it go and move on with your life. Unhealthy guilt is guilt that we refuse to acknowledge so it is unproductive, or guilt that we hold on to for too long so that it keeps us stuck in the well feeling bad and pitiful. That is self-blame and is different from taking responsibility. One keeps us stuck, the other motivates us to change. Self-blame might look good to others, but it is just another excuse to keep from being responsible."

By then the clock showed eight o'clock, so it was time to adjourn. Mike made the final comment: "Thanks for the compression check, Zeno - I guess we got our heads screwed on a little tighter tonight!"

CHAPTER THIRTEEN

Zeno began the next session by telling us about his meeting with Don King. The boxing promoter had brought ABC Wide World of Sports to the prison for a nationally televised card. I recalled the picture of Zeno with King, Joe Louis, and Larry Holmes on Zeno's nightstand. Zeno had been a contender for the middleweight crown, boxing out of Akron near King's hometown of Cleveland, and was actually on the undercard, fighting an exhibition match before the televised matches began. Zeno, who had trained only briefly before the fight, won on a third round knockout to the delight of the "hometown" crowd.

"I was feeling both incredibly excited about seeing the bouts, and very despairing about not being a part of the main events," he said. "In a way it was more frustrating to see the fights and know that I would never be a part of that scene. Don King sensed my sadness, and of all the things to say to me, he quoted Shakespeare. He told me that 'adversity is ugly and venomous like a toad, yet wears a precious jewel in its hair.'

"That night after the fighters and television people had left the prison to go celebrate together, I returned to my lock, and as I usually do when I'm feeling down, I picked up Epictetus. In one of those strange coincidences that I stopped considering coincidences long ago, I came across a passage from Epictetus that said: 'there is no such thing as being the victim of another. You can only be a victim of yourself. It's all how you discipline your mind. Show me a man who though sick is happy, who though in danger is happy, who though in prison is happy, and I'll show you a Master. So when an unwanted event happens to you, ask yourself, 'How can I use this to my benefit? What strength or personal quality is this calling for? What opportunity for self-mastery is disguised in the form of this trial?'

"I then understood what Don King was telling me – make the most of the situation you are in, look for the jewel in that ugly toad's hair. I could choose to stop feeling like a victim of what life dishes out, and decide to find a way to make my life work, whatever, whenever, and wherever I happened to find myself."

"I would hope that the toad's hair isn't as long as Don King's, or you'd never find the jewel," quipped Eddie, himself sporting quite a large Afro.

"I know you're just joking, but sometimes it does take considerable effort to sift through our circumstances to find the opportunity. You have to have faith that there is a jewel in there somewhere. Also remember that Epictetus tells us that we are never upset by our circumstances, but by what we tell ourselves about our circumstances."

Zeno then provided us with a boxing lesson. "The stance you take in the ring is very important. It will provide you with a launching pad for your punches, a cushion for absorbing the blows from your opponent, and will send a message to both you and your opponent about your toughness and determination."

He went on to demonstrate three stances. In the first stance he walked into the middle of the room with his hands down, head down, shoulders shrugged, and eyes downcast. "What do you think about this stance?" he asked the group.

"You won't get through the first round," answered Manny.

"One punch and you'll drop. You're off balance," Shakes said.

"The message you're sending is one of defeat and I think it would actually build up the confidence of your opponent," said Leonard.

"Okay, now what about this stance?" Zeno then went into a defensive posture, hands up to the side of his head, knees bent, crouched low.

"That one looks like you could take some punches," answered Eddie. "You won't get knocked down so easily. But I don't think you would win with that stance."

"Okay, now check out this last stance." Zeno then assumed a powerful stance with his hands up in front of his head, one foot behind the other, balanced, more erect, eyes straight ahead toward his imaginary opponent.

"That stance looks like you are ready for anything, and is sending a message that you are strong and confident. You can defend yourself but also counter anything your opponent might throw at you," pointed out Mike.

"Those are all very good observations," said Zeno. "We also take certain mental stances toward the events in our life. The first stance, with my hands down and eyes down, represents victim stance. The second stance, hands up to my head in the crouch, is survivor stance. The third stance represents beneficiary stance.

"Last week we talked about losing compression or power when we make excuses. The same thing happens when we see ourselves as victims of what life dishes out." He then rolled out the blackboard with the excuses still listed on them from the previous session. "Can you spot any excuses that might be described as victim stance on the board?"

"I'm a victim of my drinking," answered Shakes.

"I'm a victim of my poverty."

"I'm a victim of my parole officer."

"I'm a victim of the projects."

And on it went around the circle. Zeno then pointed out that it is possible to take a beneficiary stance toward unwanted events instead of a victim stance. "Look for the inner strength that this trial is calling forth from you. Find the not-so-obvious benefit hidden in this challenge that others, who see only in terms of good or bad, might miss."

"What good could come from growing up in the projects?" asked Leonard.

"I grew up in a tough neighborhood, too," said Eddie. "But I learned how to stick up for myself. I learned how to survive. I learned about loyalty, too. I think those are good things."

"That's the idea, Eddie. It is all in the stance we take toward events," said Zeno.

"My poverty as a child helped me learn to improvise, and it helped me to see how little one really needs to survive. I sometimes think about that to keep my desires in check."

"As for myself," said Zeno, " I came up in a tough area of Akron, and I had to fight to keep my lunch money as a kid. But I can now see that that helped me learn to defend myself, and I went on to become a fair boxer. Those skills helped me develop confidence in myself and self-control so I actually had to fight less to prove myself."

"But what about the fact that you ended up in prison? Couldn't you say that that came from having to fight as a kid?" asked Leonard.

"No, I don't think so. I am here because I turned my back on myself and on my skills and lost sight of my purpose. It wasn't confidence or boxing skills that got me here – it was losing control of myself, seeing myself as a victim of another person, instead of keeping control of myself."

Zeno then suggested that we look at this idea from another angle – from outside the box. "Think of a quality, trait or skill that you like about yourself. If you think about it, you may find that it developed out of necessity, which is sometimes just another way of saying it came from adversity."

"I think I am a patient person," said Manny. "And I can see that it was a survival tool on the rez. Things did not move too fast there, and I had to learn to wait or go crazy!"

Mike was the next to speak. "I had to learn to work on cars to keep my mom's car running so she could get to work to take care of all of us kids after dad left us. I learned I had a knack for it and soon I was working on the neighbor's car and then a lot of other cars. I see that that is a benefit that came out of our struggles to make ends meet."

"If we can look back and see how our best qualities may have come from adversity, we can learn to take that stance when difficulties arise in the present. That is what we mean by beneficiary stance. With that attitude, we are not overwhelmed by unwanted events, but we are in a strong position to come out on top," said Zeno as he assumed the strong stance he demonstrated at the beginning of the session. "Like Epictetus says, 'Assume all events happen to you for your good. All events contain an advantage for you if you look for it.'"

Animal then asked if he could share a story to wrap up the night's meeting. "Once upon a time there was a frog trapped in a well…"

"We've heard that one already," a number of voices said in unison.

"Wait a minute," advised Animal. "You haven't heard the whole story. As I was saying, there was a frog trapped in a deep dark well. He was quite alarmed so he began croaking and croaking. The farmer in the house was trying to sleep and became quite annoyed at the noise of this frog, so he decided to put a stop to it. He went to the barn and got a shovel and returned to the well. The well had gone dry and was worthless so the farmer decided to kill the frog by burying him in the well and putting an end to all the croaking. The farmer threw the first shovelful of dirt into the well, and it hit the frog, nearly panicking him. As the second shovelful of dirt landed on him, he was almost hysterical. Fortunately, this frog was a smart frog that also had read Epictetus, and he thought, 'How can I use this being buried alive to my benefit?' And then a thought struck him. Every time the farmer throws down a shovelful of dirt, I should shake off the dirt and hop up. This he did, shovelful after shovelful. The farmer was wearing himself out trying to silence that frog, but the frog just kept right on shaking off each shovelful and hopping up while he kept on croaking. Finally, the farmer had filled up the well with dirt – and the frog, who had stayed on top of the dirt all the way to the top, jumped over the wall of the well, croaked a thank you to the farmer, and hopped away."

"Another great story, Animal," said Zeno. "That is a perfect example of benefiting from adversity. Instead of being crushed, the frog was saying 'Bring it on.'"

It was now eight o'clock, so I signed the men's passes and headed for my car. My Friday night drives had become a one-man therapy session for myself, thanks to the club meetings. I was thinking about what Zeno had said about our personal strengths coming from adversity. I grew up in a family that valued athleticism, and my brother was a star high school and college player. Far from being a star myself, I was the shortest kid in my class, and had to fend for myself and develop in other ways. As a child I had shoveled snow, delivered newspapers, and done other jobs to make my own money, and later I worked my way through Ohio State by working at gas stations, pizza places, the Columbus Dispatch, and other jobs to pay tuition and rent an apartment.

What qualities did I value about myself, and had these things come from adversity and necessity? I liked my independence, compassion, sense of humor, and entrepreneurial spirit - characteristics that would serve me well as a counselor and later as a writer. Just as Zeno suggested, my childhood experiences, as difficult as they were, were indeed necessary in order for me to develop these personal qualities. I was finding myself now choosing, instead of resenting, what had happened in the past, and I better understand what Zeno meant when he told me how he did time by choosing his incarceration. I guess it's never too late to choose your childhood, either.

Anyway, life goes on. They say that a goldfish placed in a larger bowl will continue to grow. That is also true of frogs leaving wells - I grew almost a foot the year after leaving home to attend Ohio State. By the time I pulled into my driveway that night, I understood that it is hard to keep feeling like a victim when you can find benefits in a difficult situation, since it removes the sense of injury that is so necessary to feeling like a victim. Like Don King said, "Find the precious jewel in the hair of that ugly and venomous toad!"

Ribit!

CHAPTER FOURTEEN

The transfer sheet for Friday's bus trip to Lucasville arrived in the classification department Thursday afternoon. As I scanned the list, the name Scott Griswold caught my attention. That was Shakes, and he was to be on the bus Friday morning. Of course, he did not know this, and wouldn't find out until he was told to pack and report to the sally port just minutes ahead of his departure. I remembered that he was trying to earn a good conduct visit with his children, but the good time he had earned at the Walls would not transfer to Luke. I stopped by the records office and asked Mr. Schaffer, the records clerk, to pull his file. I hoped he was not close to the six-month mark needed for the visit, and was dismayed to see that he had not been written up in five and a half months. In just two more weeks he would have earned his first good conduct visit – but now that possibility was gone.

I walked across the hall to the warden's office and asked his secretary if Mr. Cartwright had a minute to see me. He heard me in his outer office and called for me to come in. "How is the Epictetus Club coming along?" he asked as I walked into the office.

"Great," I answered. "In a way, that is why I am here. Inmate Griswold, who comes to the Epictetus Club meetings, is scheduled to go to Lucasville tomorrow. He is only two weeks away from a good conduct visit with his kids. That visit is very important to him and I think it would make a big difference in his overall progress if he were able to continue to work toward it and achieve it. Is there any way his transfer could be delayed temporarily for a couple of weeks?"

The warden looked at me like I was crazy. "Are you saying that anyone who has five and a half months clear conduct record be exempt from transfer? How about five months? Four? Maybe we should just forget about transferring anyone for a while. Would you like to keep track of all that information for me so that no one close to a visit gets shipped? And please let me know whom you would replace that person with."

I remembered my "initiation," so I was ready for criticism. I simply replied, "I see your point. Sorry to take up your time, but thank you for seeing me." With that, I left the warden's office. Hopefully, I had planted a seed, but it certainly felt like I had planted it on concrete.

Friday evening I walked down to the Death House for the meeting, and was surprised to see Shakes there. I couldn't act surprised to see him, though, since his planned transfer was confidential. I secretly felt rather self-important, though. The warden must have listened to my sterling argument and seen the light. Maybe his opinion of my judgments on furlough cases would improve as well. I was now a mover and a shaker.

"Hello, Shakes," I greeted him. I then noticed that he looked a little down. "Is everything all right?"

"No, it isn't. I'm afraid I won't get my good conduct visit. I was only two weeks away from six months clear record but I got a ticket last evening. I have to appear before the Rules Infraction Board on Monday," he lamented.

"Oh, no!" I thought to myself. "Here I got the warden to pull his transfer and he gets in trouble immediately afterward. The only moving and shaking I'll be doing is if I see the warden coming!"

The meeting started promptly at seven with a quick reading of the latest framed poster on the wall:

> ## Round Five
>
> A: I'm a victim of events.
>
> B: Is this true? Where does this thought lead? Is that where I want to go?
>
> C: Assume that all events happen for my good. What benefit is hidden in this trial?

Shakes spoke first, dejectedly saying that he could see no benefit to what had happened to him. "As you all know, I have been trying to change, to be a better father to my kids. I have gotten within two weeks of a special visit, and now it's gone."

"What happened?" asked Leonard.

"I got a bullshit ticket for theft of state property last night. I found four small pieces of wood in a waste barrel that I was emptying. I took them to make a frame for something I was making and Bull busted me for it."

"What were you making?" Manny asked.

Shakes looked embarrassed, but answered anyway. "I made a painting of the Round Two poster on the wall over there, but needed a frame to stretch the canvas across." That was the poster about thinking outside the box and not giving up. " I wanted to give it to my kids on my good conduct visit. I thought it would encourage them during hard times to keep hanging in there, to find a way through their problems. And I must admit, it was something I was proud of since it was an example of my own Inner Boxing."

"Only Bull would write that ticket! That is a bullshit write-up," offered Eddie. "Did he find the wood in your lock?"

"No, it was in a common area in the cellblock."

"Then he can't prove it was yours. It could have been anyone's. Just deny it was yours." Heads were nodding in agreement with this plan.

As the complaints began growing about other perceived injustices in the institution, Zeno sympathized with Shakes, but pointed out that it was time to get the meeting started.

"Thanks for listening and letting me blow off a little steam, guys. Go ahead, Zeno, let's get going with the meeting."

The meeting proceeded with a discussion of Epictetus's statement "Do not seek to have events happen as you want them to, but instead want them to happen as they do happen, and your life will go well." As usual, the meeting broke up promptly at eight, with the men returning to their cellblock and my driving home for the weekend. I wished Shakes well as Zeno was loaning him a copy of the Epictetus handbook to read over the weekend.

Shortly after arriving at my office Monday morning I received a call from the associate warden in charge of treatment. He wanted me to sit on the Rules Infraction Board later that day. There were four cases to hear, including Inmate Griswold. "Oh, great," I thought, "the warden is really rubbing my nose in it." The Rules Infraction Board, or RIB, consisted of three staff members assigned to hear disciplinary cases within the prison. There were usually two members from the custody side and one from treatment. The members changed on a daily basis, and this was my first time on the panel.

I arrived at the correctional cells a few minutes ahead of the scheduled hearing time. The RIB met in this lowly and dank place since it was only a few steps away from where a guilty inmate might be assigned to an isolation cell. There were two officers standing by in the event an inmate took special exception to his consequence and became unruly.

Captain Meyer, who chaired the panel that day, called the first case – Inmate Scott Griswold. My very first case and I was asking to be excused from it. I explained to my fellow panelists that as advisor to the Epictetus Club I had been privy to information presented during the course of a meeting that may pertain to this case. Confidentiality was one of the rules of the group, and I felt that I was bound by that rule. Besides, if I sat on the case it would have a chilling effect on future meetings of the Epictetus Club since the men would be less likely to openly participate.

"Mr. Traylor is excused from the case of Scott Griswold for reasons of confidentiality," said the captain, speaking formally for the sake of the minutes. As an aside, he quietly added, "Please take a seat in the observation room behind us. That's a one-way glass. I suggest that you watch the proceedings so you know how the board operates. You will be hearing the next three cases with us."

After I had removed myself, Captain Meyer read the ticket out loud to his fellow panelist. It stated that four small pieces of wood, the state property in question, were found in a common area of the cellblock that had just been visited by Inmate Griswold. The state property in question had previously been in a waste barrel, and Inmate Griswold had been assigned to empty the barrel into the trash bin. The inmate had accepted the ticket in a satisfactory manner.

"What the hell is this?" commented Lt. Bell, the other panelist. "We have to find something for Bull to do to keep busy."

"Technically it is a violation. Let's see what the inmate has to say about it. If he disputes it, we'll have to back up the officer." He then called for Inmate Griswold.

When Shakes entered the room and sat down in front of the panel, he was advised that Mr. Traylor had excused himself from this hearing due to being the Epictetus Club advisor, but that the remaining two members would hear the case. In the event of a split decision, a rehearing would be scheduled with a third member present. Shakes agreed to this arrangement.

"You received a write-up for theft of state property. Did you receive a copy of the ticket?"

"Yes, sir."

"We are interested in your version of the events. What happened?"

"The ticket is right. Although it doesn't say that I had taken the wood, I did take it out of the can. I am guilty."

"Can you explain this a little more? What were you doing with it?"

"Since you ask, I'll tell you. I was making a frame for a poster I'm making for my children. I had hoped to give it to them on a good conduct visit. To be honest, I had thought about lying to you and saying the wood was not mine, but after going to a couple meetings of the Epictetus Club, I have found a new purpose in my life – being a good father. That means being a good man first of all. I could lie to you and possibly get the visit, or tell you the truth and lose the visit. I could justify either choice as being a good father, but in the end I decided to just tell the truth and leave the rest of it up to you. The wood was being thrown away, but I also understand that when the officer finds contraband, he has no way of knowing where it came from, so the rule makes sense. I felt that I was doing something harmless that was in line with a good purpose. That part was up to me and I take responsibility for it. What you do with me is up to you. I'll accept whatever you decide."

"Thank you, Inmate Griswold. Please step out for a moment while we deliberate," instructed the captain.

After Shakes stepped out, the captain turned to the lieutenant. "We rarely have any of those Epictetus guys come before the panel, but I always have the feeling afterwards that they have as much power in the hearing as we do. He took responsibility, even though it is a petty ticket. I'm for giving him one day in the c.c., but suspending it. What do you think?"

"I can go along with that," answered Lt. Bell. "Let's call him back in."

When Shakes reappeared, Captain Meyer informed him that the panel had found him guilty and assigned him one day in the correctional cell, but was suspending that day due to his attitude and demeanor before the panel.

"Thank you, sir. Is that all?" asked Shakes.

"Yes, you are free to go back to your work assignment."

After Shakes left the room, I walked out and complimented him on the way he handled himself in the hearing. He thanked me, but was obviously disappointed about losing his visit.

"I only have a minute," I said, "but I want to tell you something. Since I had been called to hear cases on the RIB, I checked out the inmate manual this morning and found this: 'Suspended sentences by the Rules Infraction Board shall not violate an inmate conduct record.' Since the board suspended your one day in the hole, you are now less than two weeks away from earning your good conduct visit with your kids."

Shakes' eyebrows shot up, a big smile came across his face, and he said, "I can't wait to share this at the next meeting. See you Friday!" With that he practically skipped down the hall to his work site.

After the next three cases were concluded, I decided to pay a visit to the warden to thank him for delaying Shakes' transfer.

"I didn't delay the transfer because of your request," barked the warden. "I had to delay it because he had a disciplinary hearing pending and we don't ship anyone under those circumstances. Since it is the holidays, there are no transfers until after the New Year. He'll be put back into the lottery until his name comes up again."

The latest words of Epictetus framed on the wall of the Death House came back to me as I left the warden's office: "Assume that all events happen to you for your good." If Shakes had not gotten that ticket from Bull, he would have already been in Lucasville and lost the visit. And if he had not taken responsibility for his part in getting the ticket, he would not have gotten a suspended sentence. As it was, everything played out just as it had to. I remembered him saying at the last meeting that he could see no benefit in his getting that write-up. Shakes would never know the details, but Zeus was clearly supporting a

man who was living in accordance with his new purpose –
being a good father.

CHAPTER FIFTEEN

The list of complaints about the prison had grown rapidly at last week's meeting after Shakes had told the men about his write-up of the night before. After sympathizing with Shakes' plight, the men began adding their own grievances to an expanding list, and with each complaint came cries of support from the others.

"We don't get enough smoke breaks," opined one man.

"We should be able to wear our own clothes," said another.

"What's up with the parole board? No one is making parole anymore."

"I don't see why we don't get more notice when we are being transferred."

"I think we should have more than two recreation periods per week."

"Why do we only get to send two letters each week? I have more family than that!"

The only thing the inmates were not complaining about was the furlough program, but that was understandable with me sitting in the room. When there was a pause in the conversation long enough for the men to catch their breath, Manny, who had been quiet until then, spoke up. "Does anyone in here remember what we talked about last week?"

"I do," answered Leonard. "Victim stance."

With that, the men began laughing, with one of them saying, "I guess that one didn't sink in, did it?"

"Don't be too hard on yourselves," interjected Zeno. "Change doesn't come overnight. It takes practice and a lot of hard work. Learning about the concept is just the first step. You need to have opportunities to apply the

91

knowledge, and then practice actually doing it. The fact that you caught yourselves at all shows good progress. Anyway, this complaining is a perfect lead in to tonight's topic - entitlement."

He then pointed out that in boxing, it is not usually one punch that takes out your opponent, but a combination of punches. "You might set him up with a jab, then follow with a cross. We do the same thing in our thinking. It is not usually just one thinking error that knocks us out, but a combination of thinking errors that takes us out. We had a good demonstration of victim stance here, and that is the set up for the next mental punch, entitlement. If I feel like a victim, then I am entitled to something, whether it be revenge, special treatment, better conditions, or just whining and complaining. This thinking error is the most painful of all of them. It causes more frustration, jealousy, and anger than almost any of the others. How did you feel while you were complaining about the prison?"

"I was getting angry," said Eddie. "And I was feeling helpless and frustrated."

"That's the point. This thinking does not get us what we want, and it only weakens us." Zeno then read a quote from Epictetus: *Do not seek to have events happen as you want them to, but instead want them to happen as they do happen, and your life will go well.*

"Basically, Epictetus is telling us to keep our expectations in line with reality, to expect the *reality* of a situation instead of its *ideal*. When we expect the ideal instead of the reality, we feel cheated and victimized. But if we ask ourselves, 'What is the nature of this?' we keep ourselves on a more even keel. For example, when we look at our complaints about the prison, Epictetus would have us ask ourselves 'what is the nature of a prison?' Are the visiting, clothing, and mail policies in keeping with the nature of a prison?"

An older convict named Bird spoke up, saying, "I noticed when the sheriff brought me here, there was a sign over the gate that said 'Ohio Penitentiary.' Right then, I figured there may be a few limitations on me. I've been in penitentiaries in three states, and I can tell you that this place is about the same as the others – which I guess means it is true to the nature of a penitentiary. I see what you're saying, Zeno - our whining is really demanding that it be something else!"

Animal then quipped, "Bird, if you've been in prisons in three states, you might want to consider getting a new travel agent!"

Bird shot a serious look at Animal, but then began laughing with the others in the group. My thoughts went to my doctor's appointment of the day before. I had sat in the waiting room about half an hour to see the doctor, and I found myself getting a little annoyed at the wait. If I had followed Epictetus's advice, I would have known that the nature of a waiting room is to wait, and especially a doctor's waiting room. Armed with that expectation, I could have taken a book to read or planned to do something else with the time instead of repeatedly telling myself, "He *should* see me now!"

"Are you saying that we should never protest anything, but always just settle for what we get?" asked Leonard.

"No, not at all. But you will think more clearly and act more efficiently if you come from a position of strength and calmness instead of upset and weakness."

Zeno then moved on to another key component of entitlement: sorting out our wants from our needs. "If you think you *need* what you are seeking, you will do whatever it takes to get it, including sacrificing something that may actually be more important to you. It boils down to this thought: I need and deserve whatever I want, and it's awful if I don't get it. And of course, I need and deserve a lot!"

"And in one lump sum, if you don't mind," added Mike to the chuckles of the other men.

"Exactly," replied Zeno. "This thinking error has us dependent on others to satisfy our so-called needs, which makes them our master and us their slave."

"I can see that in my own life," said Leonard. "I thought I needed a flashy car and nice jewelry, so I did whatever it took to get it, including selling drugs. But I traded off things that were really more important, like my family, in order to get them. If I had only thought of the car and jewelry as a want instead of a need, I don't think I would have traded off so much to get them."

"But how do you know what you need?" asked Mike.

"Bottom line, our needs are pretty basic and few. They are the things we need in order to survive – food, clothing, and shelter. Anything beyond that is a desire. The fact that we were getting upset at the beginning of the meeting about not having enough recreation periods, not wearing our own clothes, not enough mail privileges, not enough smoke breaks, and so on is a tip off that we see these things as needs, not just wants. We then compound the problem by demanding things that we not only do not truly need, but that are beyond our control to get. This is the double whammy of entitlement – 'needing' what is not within our power to obtain. If we only wanted it or preferred it, we would not be upset if we didn't have it. Or if we thought we needed it, but it was within our power to obtain, we would just obtain it. Epictetus advises us to keep it simple. He tells us, 'do your best to rein in your desires. If you desire something that is beyond your control, disappointment will surely follow. Likewise, if you resist things that are beyond your control such as illness, death or misfortune, you will also be disappointed.'"

"So my trying to resist being transferred without a two-week notice just sets me up for disappointment, since it is beyond my control," said Eddie. "I'm just giving myself a needless pain in the neck. If I saw that notice as something that would be nice, but I can live without it, I would be less stressed about the whole thing."

"Right!"

"And my trying to control what the parole board does, that can be very frustrating!"

"Yes, but if you focus on what is up to you, which is your own institutional record, you won't be frustrated, and probably more likely to make parole yourself," replied Zeno.

"I see what you're saying. But how do you handle it when you see someone else getting a better deal than you? We have a guy on our range that always gets first crack at the snacks, first choice from the book cart, and is the first to get his mail. That's not fair and it is pissing me off!" said Frank, one of the newer members.

"Are you talking about Smitty? He's such a brown noser!" said Shakes.

"Yeah, that's him – he sits there sucking up all day to the guard, getting him his coffee, listening to his family problems, even shining his shoes!"

"Then why don't you do those things, too, Frank?" asked Zeno.

"No way! I have more self-respect than that!" shot back Frank.

"That's what I thought. Let me find the passage from Epictetus that deals so well with that... Here it is: 'Has someone been given more privileges or better treatment than you? If these things are good, be glad for that person. If they are bad or could cause problems for that person, be glad they did not come to you. Remember that nothing is free, and everything has a price. Perhaps that person had to pay the price of groveling or praising someone they did not respect. Then they paid that price. You chose not to pay the price. So be it. Do not complain that they have received better things or better treatment – they bought it at a price you chose not to pay. To desire the same treatment without paying the price would be greedy and unfair.'"

"It sounds like Epictetus must have been locking with Smitty!" Shakes said.

"These human problems are timeless, whether we are in the Roman Empire or the Ohio Penitentiary," pointed out Zeno.

"I can see that our so-called 'needs' are like the attacking punches in our ABC Model of Inner Boxing, and I can see that we can block them by asking where they lead – to anger and frustration. But is there a good counterpunch to use on them?" asked Manny.

"Actually, there are two good counterpunches – and the first one is gratitude," answered Zeno. "Entitlement has us looking at what we don't have, seeing the glass as half-empty. If we can shift our focus to being grateful for what we do have, it helps us not only feel better, but also gives us something we can build on. Let's do a little exercise. Think of three things you have that you are grateful for."

Zeno picked up the chalk and began writing down the men's answers.

"I'm grateful I have my kids."

"I have my health."

"I'm still alive."

"I'm glad I get to eat every day," said Eddie, whose impressive girth supported his statement.

"I'm grateful for this group," said Manny.

"I'm glad I have a skill," said Mike.

"I'm happy that I'm clean and sober – even if I am locked up."

As the board filled up, Zeno asked the men to share any observations they might make.

"I can see that if I had kept these things in mind, and really had a sense of appreciation for them, I would not have traded them away for anything in the world," said Leonard. "The car and jewelry seem so petty beside what I had and lost."

"I feel a lot calmer and happier when I realize what I still have. Instead of whining about only getting to mail two letters each week, which is beyond my control, I can be glad that I still have someone to send them to."

"I know this might sound strange, but when I think of all the people I used to run with who are now dead, I feel pretty damn good about being locked up here. I have a second chance that they will never get," confessed Eddie.

It was getting close to eight o'clock, so Zeno wrapped up the meeting by saying that entitlement was basically demanding that things be different than they are, which generally means demanding that things beyond our control be different than they are.

"What about the second counterpunch?" asked Eddie.

"We'll start the next meeting with that one," answered Zeno. And with that the meeting broke up.

Sitting at home that night, I was thinking about Zeno's contention that gratitude was a good counterpunch to entitlement. Brand new social workers did not earn a lot of money - I was driving an old car, and my clothes, although nice, had come from a Goodwill store. I had friends who had gone to vocational school and were making more money than I was, so I felt a little on the impoverished side at times. Relaxing in my recliner, I decided to try the gratitude thing. At first I was a little stumped, but then I heard the furnace kick on. It was a cold December night, so I thought, "I'm grateful to have a furnace." As I thought about it, here I was, warm and cozy, and I didn't even have to shovel coal or chop wood. I just had to turn a dial and presto, it was warm. Then I heard the refrigerator click on, and thought, "I'm grateful for the refrigerator. Here it keeps my food cold and fresh with no effort at all from me." I turned on the radio and began listening to music. "Wow, I have bands playing for me merely by turning a knob." I then realized that the richest people in the word just a hundred years ago could not lay claim to the wealth that I was enjoying in this moment. Zeno was right – gratitude is a powerful counterpunch. I turned on the TV and kicked back in my chair, feeling like the King of England!

CHAPTER SIXTEEN

The wall behind where the electric chair used to sit was beginning to fill up with words of wisdom instead of the faces of the condemned. It now sported a half-dozen framed posters, with the latest addition reading:

> ### Round Six
>
> A: I'm entitled to have whatever I want without having to work for it.
>
> B: Is this true? Where does this thought lead? Is that where I want to go?
>
> C: I am grateful for what I have and can earn what I want.

Before the meeting began Leonard handed a folded piece of paper to Zeno. "One of the patients from Marion asked me to give this to you. He said it was from Doc."

The prison system had an underground communication network of inmates sharing information in various ways between institutions. Leonard was a porter in the infirmary, and patients who had been sent to Columbus for medical treatment at local hospitals would sometimes be confined at the prison infirmary before being returned to their home institution. Apparently Doc had sent something from Marion Correctional Institutional via a Marion inmate temporarily housed in the Ohio Penitentiary medical facility. Zeno opened up the piece of paper, which appeared to be nothing more than a newspaper article. He read it silently with great interest, and a wide smile crossed his face as he finished it.

"What's up?" asked Eddie when Zeno began refolding the paper and putting it into his shirt pocket. "I know its none of my business, but it looks like good news – and we can always use a little of that around here."

"I don't mind sharing it with you. In fact, it fits right in with what we are going to talk about tonight." He then took the paper back out of his pocket and read the article.

MCI Guard Saves Woman's Life

A Marion Correctional Institution officer was credited with saving the life of a local woman last evening after her car was struck by a Norfolk and Southern freight train at the Marion-Williamsport Rd. crossing. Twenty-seven year old Glenda Roseberry was traveling west when she apparently did not hear the warning whistle of the locomotive and drove into its path. The mother of two was traveling alone at the time. Her automobile was pushed down the tracks about 100 yards by the impact. Correctional officer John Morrison was in an automobile behind Mrs. Roseberry. After the impact Morrison ran down the tracks to the woman's car, extricated her from her wrecked vehicle and performed emergency first aid and CPR. Upon the arrival of the Marion EMS, medics took over treatment and she was transported to Marion General Hospital. This morning she is listed in serious but stable condition and is expected to survive. According to the Ohio State Highway Patrol, Mr. Morrison's swift action saved the woman's life. Morrison stated that he had just completed a CPR course at the prison earlier that evening. "I was just in the right place at the right time. I'm no hero, I just did what anyone would have done. I'm just glad I knew what to do," he told this reporter. No one aboard the train was injured, according to the state patrol.

As Zeno was refolding the paper he reminded us about Doc, with whom he had started the Epictetus Club five years ago. Doc had been transferred to Marion two years ago from the Walls. "One of the main reasons Doc wanted to go to Marion was so he could start working toward establishing first aid classes at the institution. He had been a medic in the Army, and wanted to share his skills with others. He is serving a life sentence for second-degree murder, but thought he could still be useful. We used to talk about our purpose quite a bit when we were forming the club, and whether it was possible to serve a good purpose even if you're doing a life sentence. That is when Doc got the idea to start the first aid classes.

"About a year ago he got the classes started and began training inmates. Shortly after that he offered to train the guards. He is a certified instructor and soon the guards were getting their required training from Doc. He felt like he was earning his keep that way. And as you can see from the article, it has now resulted in the saving of a young woman's life."

Everyone sat silently for several moments, thinking of the implications of this event. A man serving time for murder had now indirectly saved the life of someone else. From my conversations with Zeno, I was well aware that his thoughts were probably of Doc's atonement for his crime. While it did not bring back Doc's victim, in some way it made up for his past offense – as much as that was possible.

Animal broke the silence. "Here a woman is alive in Marion today, her kids still have a mother, and she has no idea that a prison lifer is responsible for her being alive.

There is nothing about Doc in the newspaper article. I think he should have gotten credit for it in the paper."

"I know what you're saying, Animal," replied Zeno. "But Doc will get his own personal benefit from this even if no one else knows. Epictetus taught that 'one cannot secure his own self-interest without contributing to the general welfare.' He also said 'the point is not to perform good deeds to win favor with the gods or the admiration of others, but to achieve inner serenity and thus enduring personal freedom.' The emotional relief and joy Doc is feeling must be enormous and worth more than any outside recognition could bring."

I could sense in Zeno's voice a genuine happiness for Doc even though Zeno still sought his own personal redemption. There was not a hint of jealousy in his tone.

Manny then pointed out the similarities between Epictetus's ancient Greek culture and his own Native American traditions. "Although these cultures were separated by thousands of miles, there is a similar concept in our teachings. It is called Mitakuye Oyasin, which means 'all my relatives' or 'we are all related.' You cannot harm someone else or something else without also harming yourself. Life is like a spider web, and if you harm one strand you hurt the whole web. But helping others strengthens all of the people."

"That is very interesting, Manny. We're all connected to each other in ways we can't even imagine," Zeno pointed out.

"If I might add something here, this idea is also found in eastern philosophy." The words came from Ross, who had sat quietly throughout the previous meetings. He seemed to be a pleasant young man, and was always attentive and focused. "The very act of concern for others' well-being creates a greater state of well-being within oneself, according to an ancient Tibetan tradition."

"Wait a minute – here we have ancient Greece, Native Americans, and - what did you call it? Tibetans? I didn't even finish high school and now we're talking like we're college professors!" said Animal.

Everyone laughed, but it seemed that everyone, including Animal, was also pleased with the discussion. I seldom had such engaging conversations even at Ohio State, and I told the men so.

Ross replied that he didn't learn about Tibetans in college, but had gone to the prison psychologist for help with a posttraumatic stress disorder. "I was a basket case, having panic attacks and just feeling on edge all the time. The psychologist suggested that I try meditation as a treatment for my problem, and I found it so effective that I started to study it in more detail. That is where I came across the Tibetan teachings – including the teaching on inner peace through compassion."

"I have a feeling that helping others is the second counterpunch to entitlement, after gratitude" said Eddie, gently steering us back to the main topic of the day.

"Thanks for your input, Ross. It's great to hear from you. I think you'll find this illustration right in line with your comments," said Zeno. He then picked up a piece of chalk and drew a diagram on the board:

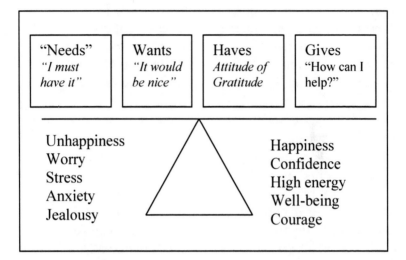

"Needs"	Wants	Haves	Gives
"I must have it"	*"It would be nice"*	*Attitude of Gratitude*	"How can I help?"

Unhappiness
Worry
Stress
Anxiety
Jealousy

Happiness
Confidence
High energy
Well-being
Courage

Zeno reminded us that last week we had talked about the attacking punch of entitlement. "I call this diagram Emotional Balance. It is like a teeter-totter. The two boxes on the left represent entitlement: my so-called needs and wants. These things keep us self-absorbed and focused on what we don't have but think we should have. The counterpunches are on the right hand side of the teeter-totter. They represent gratitude for what we have and how we can give to others and contribute to the general welfare. This is an antidote to entitlement and a path to a more peaceful life, like Epictetus and the other traditions teach."

The men sat studying the diagram for a couple of minutes, then Zeno continued. "Every time you demand something or think you need it, you are adding weight into that box. Same with your desires: if you desire or want something, like a new car or fancy clothes, you are adding weight to that box. Just like on a teeter-totter, the boxes on the ends have more effect. With more weight on the left end of the teeter-totter, you will tilt down into unhappiness, worry, stress, anxiety, and jealousy. Wants aren't as bad as 'needs,' but can still weigh us down into unhappiness. "On the other side of the teeter-totter are the counterpunches: gratitude and giving. Each time you are grateful for what you have, you add weight to that box. And each time you help someone else and contribute to the general welfare, you are adding to that box. Again, the box on the end makes the most difference. If you have more weight on the right side of the teeter-totter, you tilt into happiness, well-being, confidence, high energy, and courage." Zeno couldn't have known it at the time, but brain research that would be conducted thirty years later would confirm this very notion: the ratio of activity between areas of the brain responsible for destructive emotions and healthy emotions determined one's emotional balance and general state of happiness or unhappiness.

Animal agreed with Zeno's comments. "I've been working on the bicycle project repairing bikes from the police station to give to disadvantaged kids at Christmas. I've had to give up one of my recreation periods each week to do it, but I come away from it feeling a lot happier and calmer. And I know on Christmas day I will imagine I am in a lot of living rooms where poor kids will be squealing with excitement about their new bikes!"

"I wondered where you'd been during recreation. That's really cool," said Eddie.

There were only a few minutes left before the end of the meeting, and Zeno asked if there were any other comments. Ross asked the group members if they would like to learn a simple exercise that would help them build compassion and add weight to the "gives" box. Everyone agreed, with Leonard saying to the laughter of the others, "I would really *appreciate* it!"

"The exercise is said to have these benefits," began Ross. "You will sleep easily, you will wake easily, you will have pleasant dreams, people will love you, and your mind will be serene.

"To do the exercise, sit quietly just watching your breath as it comes and goes. Don't resist any thoughts or follow them, just observe them and let them go. Then slowly repeat these phrases to yourself:

'May I be safe and protected from all danger and harm.'

'May I be happy and peaceful.'

'May I be strong and healthy.'

'May I dwell in the ease of well-being.'

After you have repeated these phrases for yourself, repeat them for someone you care for or are grateful to, such as a teacher, mentor or spouse. Follow that by repeating them for a friend, using your friend's name, then repeat the phrases for a neutral person, such as someone you don't know but interact with on a superficial basis, such as the person scooping the food onto your plate in the mess hall. Finally, and this is the biggest challenge, repeat them for a difficult person, someone you are having trouble with, someone who you think has harmed you. Obviously this last one is tough, so don't be too hard on yourself if you can't do it. Just say the words, even if you can't feel like you mean it. Don't put any pressure on yourself to do it right, just try it as an experiment."

With that, the meeting broke up and the men returned to their cellblocks, hopefully to a good night's sleep.

CHAPTER SEVENTEEN

For the first time, one of the men in the Epictetus Club applied for furlough. Manny's kite was in the pile on my desk when I arrived at my office Monday morning. I did a cursory check to make sure he met the eligibility criteria. The next step would be to meet with him and assess his furlough plan – where he would live and work while on furlough. If everything checked out, he would be scheduled to appear before the Furlough Committee, and if approved, he would then go on to the parole board for a final determination. Manny was the seventh interview I had scheduled for Tuesday. I began the interview by asking him where he planned to live and work.

"There is a place in Columbus called the Native American Indian Center and they have agreed to help me by giving me a room in the center and a job. I would start out by helping sort donated clothing, deliver needed items to people, help with their food distribution program, and do odd jobs and maintenance work at the center. The Indian Center also offers a White Bison 12-step program that focuses on the Native American aspect of trying to heal the wounds of addiction and abuse, and I want to make that part of my furlough plan."

"Your plan sounds good, Manny. I'll have to verify it, and then you'll be scheduled for a committee hearing. I'll try to get you scheduled for the Friday meeting."

The following afternoon I drove down High St. to the Native American Indian Center. It was an unassuming two-story house that was a beehive of activity. A stately woman named Selma Walker greeted me warmly as I walked into the front room, and I immediately felt like family – Mitakuye Oyasin, I recalled, and it truly felt like it. She was the director of the center, and she verified

Manny's plan and offered to do whatever she could to help
him succeed on furlough. She would obviously be a
powerful advocate and support system for him, so I had no
qualms at all about his plan. After a very pleasant and
informative chat, I returned to the prison and scheduled
Manny for the Friday morning meeting.

Manny's case was the first one called by the
committee chairman, a review officer from the parole
authority. I presented his plan to the committee with my
observation that the plan appeared to be a good one. Manny
was called in, interviewed for a few minutes, and then he
was unanimously approved. The parole board was the next
hurdle.

The two most dangerous times for an inmate were
when they first arrived at the Walls and when they were
about to leave. They were tested upon arrival to see if they
could be intimidated or manipulated into providing goods
or services. Accepting the kindness of a seasoned convict
who offered a new arrival a pack of cigarettes soon turned
into a debt of a carton of cigarettes, with unsavory choices
sometimes being the only way to pay off this innocently
incurred debt. The men were again tested before leaving as
a kind of sport to see if they could be provoked into doing
something that would cancel their release. Misery loves
company, and for many prisoners, the more misery the
better. If someone was seen as changing his life in a
positive direction, it was quite a challenge to make it
through the final days of incarceration. He would have to
endure insults, maybe even attacks, as well as being set up
for a rule infraction by other inmates who enjoyed seeing
their peers fail. Manny had survived the entry – but could
he survive the exit?

CHAPTER EIGHTEEN

The newest poster on the wall reminded us of last week's topic – serving others as a way to inner peace. It seemed to be working for Zeno and was the key ingredient in Manny's furlough plan.

Round Seven

A: Others should serve me.

B: Is this true? Where does this thought lead? Is that where I want to go?

C: I can help myself by helping others.

After the men arrived and gave me their passes, Zeno began the meeting. As it turned out, dealing with provocation was the night's topic. I suspected that Zeno had chosen it to help his friend Manny make it through the next two weeks until the parole board met. Zeno had been around a long time, but this was Manny's first number, and by Ohio Pen standards he had done a short bit – only a little over a year, which would make him even more of a target. Zeno wanted to make sure Manny had the necessary weapons to handle being provoked.

Zeno began the discussion by revealing a little more about himself and his crime. "Before I get started on dealing with anger and hostility, I want to say a couple of things. First, maybe you are thinking that someone who is doing life for murder is not the person to be talking about anger management, and secondly, when you hear about my crime, you may think I was justified. You would be wrong on both counts.

"Twenty years ago I was dating a woman who I thought I would spend the rest of my life with. I had just asked her to marry me about two weeks before this happened. Her old boyfriend, who had never gotten over losing her, heard about it and came to our house when I wasn't there. He tried to talk her out of marrying me and to take him back, and when she refused, he beat her severely. If a neighbor had not heard the commotion and called the police, she probably would have died. When the police got to the house, the guy was gone. They called the emergency squad and then called me at the gym where I was training and told me she was on the way to the emergency room. I rushed to the hospital and couldn't believe what I saw. Here she was, a woman barely 100 pounds, beaten almost beyond recognition. Her face was cut and swollen, she was unconscious, and had tubes running into her nose and arms - all because she wanted to marry me. I lost it.

"I left the hospital and went looking for the coward who did this to my girlfriend. He was on the run and I couldn't find him at first. After about three days someone tipped me that they had seen him at an apartment building, and when I got there he was leaving in his car. I grabbed him out of the car and began beating him. I didn't stop until he wasn't moving anymore. He died right there in the parking lot. I just stood there waiting for the police. I was arrested at the scene and eventually charged with first-degree murder. At trial the prosecutor said that because I was a professional boxer, my hands could be considered lethal weapons. I was convicted and sentenced to death, spent ten years on Death Row, and then my sentence was commuted to life. And here I am."

"I would have done the same thing if somebody did that to my girlfriend. You were in the right," said Mike. Everyone else was nodding in agreement.

"No, I wasn't, Mike," answered Zeno. "It took a while for me to come to that conclusion, though. For years I believed I was justified. But when I got real with myself, I had to admit that I was not in immediate danger at the time, and neither was my girlfriend. She was under guard in her hospital room. I just wanted revenge. I spent three days looking for the guy, which ruled out self-defense. He was just a punk who could beat up a woman but not a man. The results of my actions were that I lost my freedom, my boxing career, and my girl. But my fiancé, who I thought I was protecting, lost even more. She lost her sanity as a result of what I did. There she was in critical condition, needing someone to take care of her, and that should have been me. But where was I? In the Summit County jail. She would spend the next five years scared to death, alone, and depressed. She eventually took a handful of sleeping pills. What did I accomplish? Nothing. If I would have just called the police when I got the tip about where the guy was, I might be married and have a family now. But instead, I followed the rules of the jungle and got sent to the jungle."

Everyone sat in silence at the end of Zeno's story. I know I would have wanted to do the same thing as Zeno if that happened to my girlfriend – and we were far from engaged. After a few moments, Zeno continued.

"Anger might protect us in the jungle from a real danger like a charging lion, but in modern society it cuts off our best thinking and can destroy our lives. In fact, our anger just provokes more anger in the other person, which in turn provokes more in us, in a vicious circle. If we want to stay out of the well that is the jungle, we have to master the jungle mind we are born with." Zeno spent the rest of the meeting instructing us how to do just that.

"Rarely are we confronted with situations like I just described. But we are frequently confronted with situations that if we handle poorly can escalate into more trouble than we might want, whether it is legal trouble or family or relationship problems. Feelings of anger and resentment can make our life miserable and cause physical and emotional problems. Besides, we look just plain ugly when we are upset," Zeno kidded as he displayed his wide gap-toothed smile.

"Epictetus gives us tools to deal with being angry, disrespected, or insulted. He said 'Remember that what is insulting is not the person who insults you, but your judgment about them that they *are* insulting. So when someone irritates you, be aware that you are being irritated by your own belief about the situation. Most importantly, therefore, try not to react immediately to the situation, since if you take some time and examine your thoughts you will control yourself more easily.'"

"But what if someone is verbally abusive to you? Do you just take it?" asked Leonard.

"Epictetus says that someone cannot be verbally abusive to you unless you take it that way. Otherwise it is just air blowing out of their mouth. He says we are in charge of ourselves and no one can upset us without our cooperation. This passage from the *Enchiridion* addresses that point: 'except for extreme physical abuse, other people cannot harm you unless you allow them to. And this holds true even if the other person is your parent, brother, sister, teacher, or employer. Don't consent to be hurt and you won't be hurt – this is a choice over which you have control.'"

"That sounds great – but how do you do it?" asked Shakes.

"Epictetus gives us three ways to do it: be a rock, a founding father, or a comic." At that moment Zeno unexpectedly went berserk. He turned and ran over to the coffeepot and started yelling at it. "Who do you think you are? You think you're really hot stuff, don't you? You think I'm impressed with that little red light on your side? Well, I'm not. You ain't nothin'. I've seen teapots tougher than you!"

All of us sat staring at Zeno. He appeared absolutely ridiculous and we were concerned about his sanity.

"How did I look? Tough? Intimidating?" he asked following his diatribe.

"Like a fool, or like you were out of your mind," said Animal.

"Exactly! That's Epictetus's first method – listen like a coffeepot, except he says listen like a rock, which I don't happen to have. Epictetus says 'what is this business about being insulted or disrespected? Take your stand beside a rock and insult it: what result will you get? If, then, a person listens like a rock, what does the insulter gain, except to make himself look foolish? But if the insulter has the weakness of the insulted as an advantage, then he does accomplish something.' I can tell you from the hundreds of fights I have *not* been in over the years that this works."

"I see what you mean. And that wouldn't take years of therapy to do – if I keep the rock example in mind, I won't get upset and get all the consequences that come with it. It's almost too easy!" said Leonard.

Zeno then went on to describe a second way to deal with provocation: like a founding father. "Does anyone in here know what the first amendment to the U.S. Constitution is about?"

"Freedom of speech," answered several voices together.

"Right. The ancient Greeks such as Epictetus were the originators of the idea of democracy. If you want to be able to say whatever you want, you have to give others the same right. That means that instead of thinking 'he or she shouldn't say that! Who do they think they are?' you could think instead, 'they are free to say whatever they want. They have that right. And who do they think they are? Apparently they think they are Americans, since they are saying it! I might not like what they say, but I sure like it that they are free to say it.' You'll be amazed at how much tension and stress that simple thought will remove. It takes away the struggle to try to get them not to say what they are saying. Then you can simply listen and reply, 'that is your right to say or think that. I just don't happen to agree with it.' You are actually giving them permission to say it, which is a way of having some control in the situation. You might want to refrain from using your own freedom of speech in a heated moment, though. As one guy put it, 'speak when you are angry and you'll make the best speech you'll ever regret.'"

Leonard again spoke up. "Well, that saves another year of therapy! I wish I had learned about Epictetus when I was coming up. Instead of thinking that I would be harmed by what someone said to me and then fighting to defend myself, I could have listened like a rock or just thought 'they are free to think whatever they want.'"

Before moving to the third tool from Epictetus, Zeno warned us about it. "Before you try to use this next technique in a confrontational situation, be sure you are funny and that the other person can take a joke. It involves using humor – being a comic – but if you're bad at it, you could make the situation even worse. The safest way to use it is to make fun of yourself, and not risk making fun of the other person. Here are some more words of wisdom from Epictetus: 'don't be afraid of verbal abuse or criticism. Only the weak feel compelled to defend themselves or explain themselves to others. Let your good actions speak on your behalf. We can't control the impressions others form about us, and trying to do so only demeans us. So if someone comes up to you and says so-and-so is saying bad things about you, don't get defensive and upset, but instead just reply, 'Obviously he didn't know my other bad traits, since he just mentioned these few.'" The group erupted in laughter.

"That Epictetus is a trip," said Ross. "I didn't think ancient Greeks could be so cool!"

When the group quieted back down, Zeno offered to do a demonstration. "To show you how this works, I want you to take turns insulting me. Who would like to go first?"

Stone cold silence met Zeno's request. Perhaps there is some genetic device preventing us from insulting a professional boxer serving a life sentence for murder, thereby assuring that our genes stay in the pool.

"Come on, it's OK," cajoled Zeno. "I really don't mind, and you're only doing it to help me show how it works. I promise I won't get mad – in fact, I'll enjoy it. It gives me some sparring practice so I can deal with real insulters."

"OK," said Eddie. "But I'm only kidding, you old geezer!"

Everybody, and especially Zeno, laughed heartily. He then said, "I guess I do have something to be grateful for after all – I made it to geezerdom. Thanks – you made my day!"

"Zeno, you're a punk!" There was a group-wide collectively held inhalation.

"I didn't know I still looked good enough to be a punk. Thank you!" Zeno answered.

"Man, with that space between your front teeth, you look like a beaver!"

"I know, but I can floss with a clothesline, and that is very handy!" Zeno replied.

After a few more so-called insults, the group clearly saw the point. We can't be hurt unless we consent to it, and Zeno simply refused to take us seriously. He had the power, and we looked silly and childish.

Zeno went on to caution us that while we need not react angrily to others' criticisms of us, that does not give us permission to abuse other people. "Our responsibility is still to treat others with respect, and recognize that while we may have the skills to handle these situations, not everyone does. It is in our own long-term interest to make the world as peaceful as we can for all of our sakes."

Mike then brought up a situation that he had recently been involved in. "I was on the phone and still had a minute left of my time when another inmate began pestering me to get off the phone so he could use it. He then reached over and pushed the button down, disconnecting me. I was ready to slug him when an officer walked up. If the guard had not been there, I don't know what would have happened."

"I know what would have happened," Eddie replied. "You would have gotten written up and gone to the hole, which would mean the loss of privileges, losing a good conduct visit, maybe doing more time here, or losing a transfer to a lower security prison. You could even have caught a new case for assault."

"Eddie's right," said Zeno. "You have to keep your head in these situations. One key thought to use is 'how important is this? What are the consequences? Is it worth it?' I know your call was important, but is getting that last minute more important than going home?"

"With all due respect, Zeno, you never have these kinds of problems. No one messes with you like that," Leonard pointed out. "The rest of us have to fight to keep our respect."

Zeno said that he understood. "If you remember, I used to get sent to the hole frequently for fighting since everybody wanted to prove they could beat the pro. The more I fought, the more I had to fight. I then realized that fighting wasn't getting me respect – it was getting me played. So I came up with a way to answer the instigators. I started saying to them, 'you can say whatever you want, but you won't provoke me into being the day's entertainment. I don't fight for free.'

"Of course, no one believed me at first, so they kept trying. But finally, they saw that I wouldn't react the way they wanted, and it was then that I started getting true respect. If you think about it, Leonard, you said to me 'with all due respect' a minute ago. I have never fought you, but you respect me."

"What would you have said to the guy that cut off my phone time, Zeno? Would you just let him do it?" Mike asked.

"Sometimes it is necessary to do more than just not react to something. A good place to start is to simply let the other person know that what they are doing is bothering you and ask them to stop. Sometimes they are not even aware that they are bothering you. 'Please stop talking to me while I'm on the phone, I'll be off in just a minute' is a good place to start. But sometimes you might need more if they don't stop.

"For example, I was ready with my answer about not fighting for free or being the day's entertainment," Zeno continued. "Having a 'go-to' thought is helpful in these kinds of situations. Let's try to think of a response ahead of time that shows that you will stick up for yourself, but is not something that will further heat up the situation."

The men sat pondering the problem for a few minutes, and then Eddie spoke up. "What about saying to the guy, 'retaliating against you is tempting, but not as tempting as going home to my family.'"

"That's a good one, Eddie. It shows you are being reasonable, not afraid," replied Zeno. "It may even remind the other guy of his own possible losses. Any others?"

Shakes provided the next example: "I see that you are counting on one of us to have some common sense here, so I'll be the one and save us both a lot of trouble by walking away. Next time it will be your turn."

"Nice job, Shakes. That has some humor and also has you both on the same team."

"You could say, 'please back off – we're both having bad days, but tomorrow will be better,'" offered Animal.

"Those are all good," Zeno replied. "It is better to use your brains and your creativity instead of your fists – and you can take that from someone who learned it the hard way!"

We were near the end of the session, and Manny offered to share a joke that he learned back on the reservation. "You all know about the Lone Ranger and his faithful Indian sidekick, Tonto? Tonto used to call the Lone Ranger 'Kimosabe' in the most respectful and serious tone. After the Lone Ranger retired, he moved to a retirement home and one day he was playing shuffleboard. Another old guy who used to be a veterinarian said, 'Man, I'm glad I don't have to look at any more kimosabes.'

"'What do you mean?' asked the Lone Ranger. 'My faithful sidekick Tonto used to call me 'kimosabe.'

"'Oh, I'm sorry to tell you this,' replied the vet, 'but kimosabe is a veterinarian's term for horse's ass.'"

That brought hearty laughter, and with that the meeting broke up. I never would have guessed that a session dealing with insults could be so much fun.

Over the weekend I had my own opportunity to try out Zeno's teachings. I stopped at a garage to have my oil changed, and the mechanic showed me my dirty air filter and said he could replace it for only $15.00. I couldn't afford it, so I said, "No thanks." He then said I was making a very bad move, looked at me with disdain, shook his head and walked away, muttering, "That's really stupid."

Instead of arguing and getting angry, I was polite and agreed with him. Recalling that he has freedom of speech, I called out, "You're right, it is stupid - and that's not even the stupidest thing I've done today!" That was met with a moment of silence, then a laugh and a thank you for my business. I then drove across the street to a parts store, bought a filter for $5.00 and installed it myself in thirty seconds. Dealing with the rudeness was totally effortless, just like Leonard had suggested. I spent a peaceful weekend just wishing someone else would insult me, but, alas, everyone seemed kinder than usual.

When Monday morning rolled around, I went to the office and discovered that I had mistakenly left someone off the pass list, which meant I had to run the inmate's pass over to Big Block myself. After handing the pass to Bull, who was having his shoes shined by inmate Smitty, I saw Manny and Animal walking toward me along the range. We exchanged greetings as we passed, and I turned the corner to go down the stairs. It was then that I heard a voice say, "Well, if it isn't the little 'injun' that could. I hear you made it past the furlough committee." The voice belonged to Bull, and it was soon joined by Smitty's voice saying, "You're not out yet, Geronimo."

I stopped to sip my coffee and listen. Manny did not respond but had attempted to keep walking past this potentially dangerous situation. Bull ordered him to stop and said, "I'm talking to you, boy. You better show me some respect if you ever want to get out of here."

"Yes, sir," replied Manny. I could feel the tension as the hairs on the back of my neck stood up. I knew Manny's furlough was on the line.

Smitty, presented with an irresistible opportunity to curry even more favor from the officer, said, "I don't think that's good enough. Try it again, Tonto. What do you say to the man?"

Manny stood silently for a moment, with Animal shifting uncomfortably at his side. Manny, looking from Bull to Smitty and then back to Bull, finally said in a calm and absolutely sincere voice, "Yes, *Kimosabe*." It was all I could do to keep from blowing my coffee out through my nose.

"That's better. Now get out of here," ordered Bull, unaware that he had just fallen into his own trap. Manny and Animal wasted no time hustling away.

After that episode, I was more comfortable than ever with the committee's decision to furlough Manny. Two weeks later the parole board agreed. To my knowledge, Bull was the only one who tried to provoke Manny during those two weeks. It would be several months before I found out that Zeno had put out the word in the prison that no inmate was to touch Manny. Zeno was one of only a handful of inmates who had that kind of juice – but of course he couldn't control what Bull would do. Manny showed his true warrior skills by handling that one himself. Perhaps Zeus (or one of his agents) was watching - strangely enough, Bull did not return to work again due to an "administrative issue."

When the day came for Manny to leave, I escorted him and the three other furloughees to the bullpen to hand them off to the outside furlough officer. As he passed through Zeno's gate on his way to freedom, I heard Manny say, "Mitakuye Oyasin."

"Mitakuye Oyasin," Zeno replied. "Good luck to you, my brother."

CHAPTER NINETEEN

It had been three weeks since the last Epictetus Club meeting. With the Christmas and New Year's holidays falling on Fridays, there were no meetings. It felt good to be back together – but Manny's absence was noticed, even though everyone was happy that he was "outside the well." The new poster on the wall reminded us of our last session:

Round Eight

A: He can't say that to me!

B: Is this true? Where does this thought lead? Is that where I want to go?

C: He has freedom of speech – he can say whatever he wants. In fact, I give him permission!

Zeno welcomed us back and hoped that we had had a good holiday – at least as good as possible under the circumstances. As a special holiday treat for the inmates, the men had been allowed to go to the mess hall for a special showing of that holiday classic *Magnum Force* starring Clint Eastwood as Inspector "Dirty Harry" Callahan, who had made the line "go ahead, make my day" famous. Consequently, all week we had endured Dirty

Harry impersonations. But tonight Zeno asked if anyone remembered the closing line that Clint Eastwood uttered in *Magnum Force* as he watched the villain drive away and blow himself up.

In his best squinty-eyed, even-toned voice, Mike growled out the words, "A man's got to know his limitations."

It was a passable rendition that was greeted with laughter from the men and a compliment from Zeno. "Nice job, Mike. And that is the topic of tonight's meeting of the Epictetus Club."

Zeno then went on to share a passage from Epictetus that reflected Dirty Harry's sentiments: "Understand what freedom really is and how it is achieved. Freedom isn't the right or ability to do whatever you want. Freedom comes from understanding the limits of our own power and the natural limits set in place by divine providence. By accepting life's limits and inevitabilities and working with them rather than fighting against them, we become free.'

"Limits and freedom seem like opposites, but they actually work together. When we don't understand this, we get in trouble, but when we do understand it we gain personal freedom and increased efficiency and effectiveness. We don't waste time on what is beyond our limits, and we don't arrogantly overestimate our skills and abilities. This is the core of the number one thought that brings people to prison: 'I won't get caught because I'm too slick.' But the fact of the matter is we get caught every time."

"I gotta disagree with you on that one, Zeno," said Leonard. "I committed a lot of crimes that I got away with. In fact, I got away with a lot more than I got caught for."

"I don't disagree with that, Leonard, but the fact that you are here means you did get caught for something. I maintain that we are here for everything we have ever done. Let me ask you this: what happened when you got away with a crime? Did getting away with it make you stop doing it – or did it just encourage you to do it again?" asked Zeno.

"It encouraged me to do it again."

"And how long did you keep doing it?"

"Until I got caught," Leonard sheepishly answered. "I see what you mean. Getting away with crimes just kept me doing crimes until I did get caught, and now I'm paying all those prices I put in my circles a few weeks ago."

Zeno then asked the group, "When do you know you have gotten away with a crime?"

"When I get out of the building," said one man.

"When I get home safe," said another.

"I worry for a couple days, but then it goes away and I don't sweat it any more," answered a third.

"That's what I used to think, too," said Ross, and he went on to describe his arrest. "It had been five years since I had been part of an armed robbery that netted us a few hundred dollars. I had honestly only done that one crime. Five years later I was going to Ohio State and living a responsible life. I was on a city bus traveling down High Street when two detectives came on the bus at 15th Avenue and asked me my name. When I answered, they cuffed me and took me off the bus. As it turned out, one of the people I did that crime with had gotten himself arrested and gave me up for a better deal. Even though I had changed my life, my rappie hadn't, so here I am. So to answer your question, Zeno, you never know."

Everyone sat silently for a few moments, then Zeno spoke.

"You make a very good point, Ross. Unfortunately, we cannot undo the past and our past actions, but we can cut our losses in the present and create a better future for ourselves. The next time we think about committing a crime, we might ask ourselves, 'what will I be doing five years from now? How old will my kids be? What if I have a good job and am doing well? Would I want to lose it all for the sake of this crime I am thinking about committing? You aren't just risking your present situation, but your future as well. Do you want to risk the happiness of your future self and family for this? Do you want it hanging over your head forever? If not, then don't do the crime.'"

Zeno then opened a dog-eared copy of the complete works of Ralph Waldo Emerson and read a paragraph that that champion of liberty and personal freedom wrote a century and a half earlier. "Commit a crime and the earth is made of glass. There is no den where the rogue can hide. Commit a crime, and it seems as if a coat of snow fell on the ground, such as reveals in the woods the track of every fox and squirrel and mole. You cannot take back a spoken word, you cannot pull up the ladder so as to leave no clue. Some damning evidence always transpires to become a penalty to the thief."

Zeno paused as the words of Emerson sunk in.

"Wow," said Mike. "Emerson wrote that before there were even things like fingerprints to solve crimes." He then made a comment that would come true many years later with the development of DNA analysis: "Who knows what may come up in the future to solve crimes that are even decades old!"

"If we know this, and respect this, we will not step past these limits and into trouble," Zeno added. "As Epictetus said, by working with these limits instead of against them, we become free."

All the men in the group were nodding in agreement as they looked at their own situations. I was thinking about the number of men I had spoken to who had been caught selling drugs, and it occurred to me that if a person sold drugs to ten people, and those ten people each told ten other people where they got their drugs, 110 people would know. If any one of those 110 people got caught for something, which was highly likely, they could cut a deal by giving up the seller. It looked like Emerson was right indeed!

Zeno then said, "Not only do we think we won't get caught, but we have ways of thinking that we are good guys while doing these bad things. I call this the Saint Hood Syndrome," he said, drawing laughter from the group.

"You all know the story of my crime," he continued. "I told myself that I was protecting my girlfriend, that I was doing it for her – that I was Saint Zeno. That thought was a punch that helped knocked me out."

"I hear other convicts describing the 'best' way to do a crime, or how to do the job 'right,' and so forth. Is seeing crime as a 'skill' or as a 'success' also part of Saint Hood?" asked Animal.

"I think so," replied Zeno. "Calling it a skill or our work or our job just leads us down the road to eventually getting caught and locked up. If we keep it real, we know crime is not a skill or a job – it is nothing but a crime. And this truth will help keep us free in the future by not letting us get over on ourselves like we're doing a good thing when we're actually hurting others. There is no 'good' way to do a bad thing, no 'right' way to do a wrong thing, and no 'smart' way to do a stupid thing."

"I thought I was getting more skillful and smarter as I went along, but I can see that I was just getting arrogant and careless from my so-called successes while setting myself up for failure and misery," pointed out Mike.

"Now I see why Robin Hood had to have his motto: Steal from the rich to give to the poor. That made it seem like a good thing, even though he probably kept most of the loot for himself," chimed in Shakes.

"I know I felt better about my crimes when I said I was supporting my family, but I was really just looking for a fast and easy buck. And now I'm giving my wife and kids the big bucks, alright!" said Eddie, referring to his prison pay. Inmates who had work assignments were paid at the rate of five cents per hour, or if they had verified dependents like Eddie, made 9 1/2 cents per hour. Of that, 4 1/2 cents were sent to the inmate's dependents. Full time prison labor resulted in $27 being sent to the family every three months by the cashier's office.

Zeno asked if anyone else could identify any Saint Hood thinking that they had engaged in that helped them feel like they were good guys while doing bad things.

"I told myself that the people I sold drugs to were my customers, and that they were doing this by choice. In fact, I even gave them free Thanksgiving turkeys, just like any other business. In reality they and their families were my victims and I was preying on their addiction."

"I always was sure to put money into the kettles at Christmas time. That helped me seem like a good guy."

"I would give my wife flowers and candy on Valentine's Day to make myself look like a great husband, then run around on her the rest of the year. If she got upset about something, I would remind her what a great guy I was."

After a few more examples from the group members, it was time for the meeting to come to a close. Shakes asked, "Is there a good counterpunch to the attacking thought 'I won't get caught?'"

"There are four little words that will keep you out of jail, and if you adopt them as your motto they will keep you free. Don't argue with them, or make exceptions. You might even want to tattoo them on your forehead in reverse so they are the first things you see when you look in the mirror in the morning. These four magic words of freedom are these: *I will get caught!*"

"Simple but effective," responded Leonard. "I can remember those easily enough!"

As the men filed out of the little brick building, Mike turned to Zeno, squinted, and growled, "Thanks – you made my day."

CHAPTER TWENTY

The bus trips to Lucasville had resumed again, placing an added strain on both staff and inmates. The tension in the prison was at a fairly high level, so everyone in the group was pleased that dealing with stress would be the night's topic. Zeno pointed over to the new frame on the wall, which highlighted last week's lesson, before beginning the night's discussion.

Round Nine

A: I'm invincible, unbeatable, and I'm too slick to get caught.

B: Is this true? Where does this thought lead? Is that where I want to go?

C: I will get caught!

"What are some of the things that cause you the most stress, things that you worry about?' Zeno asked to begin the session.

"I worry about my parole hearing this spring," answered Leonard.

"I'm worried about my transfer to Lucasville," replied Juan, a new member of the group.

"I worry about my kids," said Shakes. "But I had a great visit with them last week for my good conduct visit, and I feel a little better now."

"I worry about death," admitted Eddie.

"I worry about my wife's finances while I'm here," Mike said.

"I worry about getting a job when I get out of here," Animal replied.

As the men were giving their answers, Zeno was writing them on the chalkboard. After the list had grown to fill the board, he stepped back and said, "There are so many things to worry about. In fact, I can think of only two things in the world *not* to worry about." He then just stood there, waiting on the obvious question.

"Well, aren't you going to tell us what those two things are?" asked Mike.

"They are the things we can do something about, and the things we can't," he answered.

The men sat pondering for a moment, and then the usually quiet Ross spoke. "I know what you mean. If we can do something about it, then do it. If we can't, what good is it to worry about it?"

"That's right," said Zeno. "The very first words in *The Enchiridion* are 'some things are up to us and some things are not up to us.' This is the cornerstone of inner peace for Epictetus."

"That sounds like a short version of the Serenity Prayer that we recite in our AA meetings," observed Animal.

"Yes, it is the same idea," answered Zeno. He then erased the board and wrote the letters CALM. "When you are worried or upset about something, you can use the CALM model to be less anxious. We can all remember to think CALM in the midst of emotional turmoil. Each letter represents a step on the pathway out of the stress. C stands for *cognition*, which is just a fancy word for thinking. Ask yourself, 'Is this up to me or not up to me?' According to Epictetus, the things that are up to us include our opinions, desires, and attitudes. I would also add our choices and actions. Things that are not up to us include what other people say or do, our bodies, our possessions, our health, our death, and even our reputations. Although we can certainly influence these things, in the last analysis, they are beyond our control. We can get diseases, others can slander us, our things can be stolen, and we can lose a prestigious job if a company closes – or, in our case, if a penitentiary closes. If we have mistakenly attached ourselves to these things that lie outside of our control, we have set ourselves up for a hard fall.

"The second letter in CALM is A, which stands for *act*. If you answered that the thing you are worried about is up to you, then do what you can do about it. Break it down into small steps if necessary, but begin by taking a positive action that will help bring about the desired result. Put one foot in front of the other and keep going. Action tends to reduce worrying and increase efficiency.

"If you answered that the thing is not up to you, go to the next letter in CALM, which is L, meaning *'let it go.'* Find a way to accept what is happening without causing you anxiety, fear, or undue stress. Epictetus suggested that we learn the art of indifference toward things that are not up to us. Just turn your thoughts to other things and don't give it any more energy. This is actually easier than you might think. Tell yourself 'this too shall pass,' or perhaps 'it's none of my business.'"

Zeno then moved on to the last letter in CALM. "Finally, the last letter is M, for *'move on'*. Don't spend your time dwelling on things beyond your control, move on to something else. And it usually doesn't take too long for the next thing to arise."

At this point Ross asked if he could share a story that might help all of us with the letter L, the notion of "letting it go." "One time there was a man named Milarepa who lived quietly in a cave where he spent the days meditating. One day he went out to gather firewood, and when he returned there were a bunch of demons in his cave. They had just moved in, were eating his food, messing up the place, making noise, and generally being a real nuisance. He ran at them, screamed at them, and threw things at them to try to get them to leave. Nothing worked. He tried reasoning with them. That didn't work either. Finally, he decided that since he wasn't going anywhere, and they weren't going anywhere, they would all just have to get along and share the cave. At this, much to Milarepa's surprise, all the demons except one left the cave. This last demon was a particularly fierce-looking one with a huge mouth and sharp teeth. Rather than fighting with this last fierce demon, Milarepa simply decided to crawl into its huge mouth and offer himself to it completely. It was then that even this last demon left.

"The lesson of this story is this: when the resistance is gone, so are the demons. This story works for me. In any situation where I truly have no control, I crawl into the situation's mouth and just relax. I tell the demon to do what it will, I'm not going to get into a useless and futile fight, and my stress almost always disappears," Ross said, "but that only applies after you have done what is up to you, as Epictetus would put it."

132

"I think Epictetus would have liked that story. It seems to fit right in with his teachings. He would have seen the resistance as craving something beyond our control, and when we give that up, we have peace," Zeno pointed out.

We then turned our attention to the blackboard and used some of the items on the board to practice applying the CALM model. We started with Leonard's concern about the parole board.

"Start with C, your *cognition* or thinking. Is what the parole board does up to you or not?" asked Zeno.

"Well, I guess part of it is up to me and part of it isn't. I'm not in charge of what their decision is, but I am in charge of part of it – like my institutional record, for example."

"That's a nice job of sorting it out, Leonard. You have both elements. Now we'll look at the next letter: A. For the part that is up to you, what *action* can you take?"

"I can make sure I don't break any rules and get written up for it. I can attend all of the groups like this one and AA that will help me learn to solve my problems. And I can work to get a good report from the laundry supervisor where I work."

"Great job. Now for the part of it that is not up to you – which is whatever decision the parole board makes – what can you do?"

"I can remind myself that that is not up to me, and practice acceptance. I can just shift my thoughts to things that I can do something about. When I start worrying about the board, I can go play cards or basketball," replied Leonard.

"Who wants to go next?" asked Zeno, and several hands shot up. "Mike, do you want to go ahead with your worry about your wife's finances?"

"OK. Is it up to me? No, I'm not out there, so there is nothing I can do."

At this point, Shakes asked Mike if he could suggest something that might help and would be something that was up to Mike. Mike said it would be OK. "Does your wife send you cigarettes?" asked Shakes.

"Yes, about a carton a week," answered Mike.

"My wife used to send me cigarettes, too. But when I thought about it, I realized that that is an expense she doesn't need. I also realized that my kids could use that money for school clothes, so I had her stop sending me smokes. It hasn't been easy," he said, displaying severely chewed fingernails to the laughter of the others. "But when I remind myself that I am doing it for my kids, it is really a lot easier than I thought it would be. It is in line with my purpose of trying to be a good father to my kids, even if I am in here, and that brings me some peace – even while I'm jonesing for some tobacco."

"I see your point, Shakes. Maybe I could try that, too," Mike said with less than overwhelming conviction.

"That demonstrates how important it is to sort accurately between what is up to us and what is not up to us. It comes with practice," Zeno added. "Juan, you listed something that is on the minds of a lot of us – our transfers out of here to Lucasville, or wherever we might be sent. Let's break that one down by starting with C in CALM: Is our transfer up to us or not up to us?"

"I would have to say it is not up to us," replied Juan. "And since it is not up to us and therefore there is nothing we can do about it, we can go past the A in CALM to the L, let it go. I could just say to myself, 'no point in worrying about it. It will happen when it happens. I'll just have to be ready to go when they say, and then M, move on to something else."

"I think that is the best way to deal with it, Juan," replied Zeno to the nodding agreement of the others.

"What about death and pain?" asked Eddie.

This was a question that everyone in the room was thinking about, and Zeno had obviously checked out Epictetus on the subject. Although no one had specifically mentioned it, there was a subdued sense in the room this night. It had been just one day since a fatal stabbing had taken place in the prison – in fact, just outside the door of my office in the classification department. An inmate had gained access to the area using a fake pass and had stabbed one of our inmate clerks to death with a homemade shank. Apparently the victim had failed to repay a debt of a bag of potato chips on time, and it had cost him his life. Although this happened occasionally at the pen, it was the first time it had happened since I started working there, and its proximity to me had me also searching for a way to view death and mortality.

"Epictetus reminds us that death and pain are inevitable things," Zeno said. "He advises us not to dread death and pain, but to dread the *fear* of death and pain. He emphasizes that it is our *notions* that terrify us, not death and disease and pain themselves." I was reminded of my first visit to this very room, when the electric chair had un-eased me while Zeno was calm and relaxed. "Epictetus says not to get too attached to our bodies, since they are temporary things, and that is their nature. We are mortal. He likens our bodies to a room at an inn. We live in it for a while and then move out. But some people who fear death and aging do more than just keep their room orderly and clean – they completely redecorate and remodel their motel

135

room and spend an excessive amount of time and money worrying about their temporary quarters. If you think about it, there is a huge industry in this country that plays on our fear of illness and death, of something that is inevitable. Watch TV for a while, and you will see that the ads are almost all for drugs to try to keep us living forever. They play on our fears of the inevitable. They tell us that aches and pains are awful and can be avoided by taking a pill, which sends the message that drugs are the answer to all of life's problems and inconveniences. Ironically, our fear and resistance to the physical sensations we call "pain" actually make the sensations more intense. You can check this out for yourself when you leave the meeting tonight. Instead of hunching up and steeling yourself against the cold and wind blowing across the yard, try relaxing into it by dropping your shoulders and not concentrating on the sensations so much. You'll find that after you absorb the initial chill, you will be *less* cold.

"Epictetus would say that it is better to live in peace in the present, pursuing our purpose in life, rather than waste our time fearing something beyond our control – like death or illness. Do what you reasonably can to be healthy and to protect yourself, but realize that in the end, the end is not up to us. In fact, the happier we are, the healthier we are and the less likely we are to need all the stuff being advertised. Epictetus himself was said to be lame and in poor health most of his life, but he was happier than most of us today. He realized he was more than just his body."

"That helps a lot, Zeno, but I have one question about it. If we don't worry about something, does that mean we don't care about it? I care about making parole, about my transfer, and about my health," said Mike.

Zeno made a distinction between worry and concern. "Concern, or caring, motivates us to do something in situations that are up to us. It is like an alarm clock – it wakes us up and we act. Worry, on the other hand, is like the alarm clock ringing, but not ever turning it off. It just keeps ringing and we keep fretting. Concern is useful, worry is counterproductive"

We were running out of time, so Zeno wrapped up the meeting by briefly telling us about syllogisms, or arguments that the ancient Greeks constructed to prove or disprove something logically. He wrote the four possible combinations of worry and outcomes on the board, and then shared his comments about each possibility.

1. I worried and the feared thing did not happen. "In this case, it was wasted worry. Like Mark Twain said, 'My life has been filled with disasters, most of which never happened.'"

2. I worried and the feared thing did happen. "At first you might think, 'See, I was right to worry.' But what better argument against worry is there? It did not keep the unwanted thing from happening, so it is an ineffective way to deal with it."

3. I did not worry and the feared thing did not happen. "Good, we had peace of mind here and no wasted energy."

4. I did not worry and the feared thing happened. "Worry does not magically prevent unwanted things from happening. This person did not deplete himself or herself with worry so they have more strength to deal with the problem and its solution."

It was now eight o'clock, so the meeting was adjourned. Zeno bade us goodnight and we all headed to our temporary quarters – the inmates to their cells and I to my apartment. I was unaware that I had just attended my last Epictetus Club meeting. That night on my drive home I was thinking how much I enjoyed my job, and that I was worried that I would soon be losing it. Funny, the temporary nature of it had attracted me to begin with, and now I was worried about its very temporariness.

But why would I want to keep working here – or any place like it? I had already been asked that question numerous times by friends, family and strangers in the few months I had been working at the Walls. It was not a bad question. People getting killed over a bag of potato chips, nighttime phone calls about escaping convicts, rampant unkindnesses in a hostile environment. As I reflected on the question, it occurred to me that maybe I liked it for the same reason that I was inspired by the sight of a weed struggling up through a crack in the sidewalk, or a daisy growing in a dusty, abandoned lot. It was not a feeling of pity for the flower, but an admiration for the latent strength it represented in all of us, an ability to overcome our circumstances, to rally ourselves against stagnating forces - whether it be other convicts afraid of change or our own internal negative monologue - the determination to not give up, to keep trying. The penitentiary was clearly an arid environment, but here and there a few green shoots like the men of the Epictetus Club sprouted, powered by their own internal drive toward change, and I wanted to be a part of that process for as long as I could.

But Epictetus said change was a basic characteristic of life itself, and the sooner I accepted that fact the better off I would be. Think CALM, I reminded myself - I'd just do my job to the best of my ability, enjoy it while I had it, and leave the rest to Zeus. As Zeno had said at one of our earliest encounters, "all things must pass" – even penitentiaries.

CHAPTER TWENTY-ONE

Monday morning I received a call from the warden. He asked me to come to his office right away. When I arrived he informed me that due to the closing of the penitentiary, I was not to accept any more furlough applications. "The inmates can apply at their new institutions," he said. "In the meantime I want you to start closing up your files and packing away your office after you take care of this last piece of business." He handed me a piece of paper, which for all practical purposes represented my pink slip. "When you're done with that, see if the other social workers need any help from you." I felt stunned – I knew this was coming, but still I hadn't expected it so soon.

I left the warden and started walking toward my office. As I passed through Zeno's gate, he asked to speak to me for a moment. "With the penitentiary closing down, guys being shipped out, and who knows how long before we lose our Club advisor," he said smiling, "I think it is time for me to apply for furlough. I said I hoped I would know when it was time to move on, and this is it. I feel really good about what I have been able to do with the Epictetus Club, and I want to keep doing it. I've arranged a plan where I can live at the halfway house in Columbus and work with newly released inmates who are staying there. Manny and I might even be able to do some programs together," he added happily. "I waited until today so I could give you my kite in person." As he started to hand me the kite, my heart sank.

"Zeno, I'm sorry. We've stopped taking furlough applications. You can apply when you get to your new institution." I couldn't bear to look at Zeno's face, so I kept on moving through the gate.

When I reached my office, I sat down at my desk and looked out through the bars on my window. I could just see the top of a railroad bridge beyond the wall, and I sat staring at it. Now that I was to stop processing furlough cases, I really had no job. How much longer would I be here? What would I do? How would I survive? I had been here such a short time that I didn't even qualify for unemployment benefits. I could feel myself getting panicky, but then I remembered to think CALM. I worked my way through the letters, finally saying to myself, "Worry won't help, it is out of your hands, just let it go and move on."

I also recalled how the Prayer of Epictetus had helped me in the hills of Pennsylvania when Crime Wave had escaped, so I recited it to myself once again: 'Lead me, Zeus and Destiny, whithersoever I am appointed to go. I will follow without wavering; even though I turn coward and shrink, I shall follow all the same.' If Zeus wants me out of here, I would just have to go. I felt myself relax while I was shrinking a little less rapidly. The phone rang a few minutes later, and it was the warden. "Sorry to bother you again, Traylor, but could you please come back to my office. There is someone here who wants to speak to you."

I dreaded passing through Zeno's gate again, but it was necessary in order to get to the warden's office. As I walked by, Zeno said reassuringly, "Don't worry, everything will turn out OK." I had the feeling he wasn't just talking about his situation, but was sharing his concern for me as well. He obviously realized that if there were no more furlough cases, there would be no more furlough counselor.

"Thank you, Zeno. Let's hope so," I replied.

When I walked into Mr. Cartwright's office, I saw that another man was sitting across the desk from the warden and they were engaged in a friendly conversation. "Come in, Jeff, I want you to meet someone. This is Pete Perini, the superintendent of Marion Correctional Institution."

Mr. Perini stood up, smiled, and reached out a massive hand to greet me. He was a bear of a man, a former pro football lineman, with a friendly face and easy smile. "I would like to talk to you about coming to work for me at Marion. We need to get our furlough program off the ground, and I noticed that you've sent more candidates to the parole board than we have – and you're the max prison. That makes us look bad," he joked, referring to Marion's medium security status. "Warden Cartwright even had some good things to say about you. Would you consider coming to MCI and being the furlough counselor?"

I could feel the load lift off my shoulders. I liked Mr. Perini and was excited that I could continue working in corrections. I immediately said, "When would you like me to start?"

"The warden says you're finished with your cases here, so could you start next week?"

I looked at Mr. Cartwright and he nodded his approval, saying he could take me off his payroll at the end of the workday on Friday. "I'll see you Monday - if you tell me how to get there," I answered. We shook hands, I thanked both men, and almost floated out of the warden's office. As I approached Zeno's gate, I came back to earth again. "Zeno, I've accepted a new job at MCI. My last day here is Friday at the end of my regular shift, so I'm afraid I won't be here for any more meetings of the Epictetus Club."

"That's great news! When you get to Marion, be sure to look up Doc and tell him I said hello." I sensed the same equanimity in him that he displayed when the Epictetus Club lost the chaplain as its advisor and it looked like the club was finished. There was not a hint of jealousy or bitterness, either – just happiness at how things were working out for me. I only wished things were working out better for Zeno.

I began clearing out some drawers and putting things in boxes. When I started on the desktop, I noticed the piece of paper that the warden had given me earlier that day – my "pink slip." In my worry, I had forgotten to look at it. I unfolded it and read that the warden was initiating a furlough for an inmate who had not applied. As the head of the institution, the rules gave the warden that authority. This was the first time it had been used, however. In the view of the warden, the inmate had done exceptionally well in the prison, had served sufficient time, and further incarceration would serve no useful purpose. Therefore, Mr. Cartwright was recommending to the committee and parole board that Zeno be furloughed at the soonest possible time.

I rushed down to Zeno's gate and told him that he would be appearing before the furlough committee on Friday – thanks to the warden. "And maybe thanks to Zeus, too," he happily added.

As it turned out, Zeno was the only case we heard on my final day at the Walls. He was unanimously approved, and went on to be unanimously approved by the parole board. The last I heard he was doing well at the halfway house and had begun an Epictetus Club for not only residents of the house but anyone who wanted to come. As for me, when the furlough committee meeting ended, I went back to my office and finished packing up. At the end of the day, I carried my box out through Zeno's gate, exchanged goodbyes and good lucks, and left the Ohio Penitentiary behind. When I got home and began unpacking my stuff, I found a frame that I had not put in the box. It is hanging over my desk today as I write these words:

Round Ten

A: I must worry and be anxious about events.

B: Is this true? Where does this thought lead? Is that where I want to go?

C: Be CALM. Some things are up to us, and some things are not up to us.

Thanks – The Epictetus Club

EPILOGUE

It had been almost three decades since the men of the Epictetus Club had gone their separate ways. Now, the long-abandoned prison was being demolished to make way for an arena for the new Columbus National Hockey League franchise. The walls had already come tumbling down, and as I stood across Neil Ave. with my wife I could see the shell of Big Block still standing, having absorbed several blows from the huge wrecking ball that was tearing down the prison. It was an extremely eerie sight, with the six tiers of cells smashed open to the light of day. Things were revealed to outside eyes that had not been seen for a century and a half. Somehow it almost seemed like an invasion of privacy of the men who had lived, and died, within those confines.

In the intervening years, I had gone on to work at Marion Correctional Institution, community mental health centers, and then left the system altogether to write a series of Ohio travel books called *Life in the Slow Lan e*. But Mr. Burkhart was right – I did have correctional fluid in my veins, and after fifteen years of traveling the back roads, I had recently returned to corrections to teach cognitive skills classes at a community-based correctional facility in Tiffin, Ohio. I was now the age that Zeno had been when I started at the pen, and my own hair had turned gray. He was probably dead by now. My thoughts drifted back to the men from the Epictetus Club. As I was telling my wife about the prison and the Club, about Zeno, Shakes, Animal, Leonard, Manny, Eddie, Mike, and the others, an elderly man approached. He stood for several minutes, just staring at the scene, his mind seemingly adrift in the past. To be friendly I finally broke the silence. "Heck of a place, isn't it?" I said.

"Yes, it is," he said. "If we didn't know better, it would be hard to tell if it was a castle to keep people out or a prison to keep people in."

The next words he spoke sent chills down my spine. "But I guess it is like life, you can either make it a palace or a prison. It's all in what you tell yourself." And with that he winked at me and walked away. I swear I noticed a slight limp as he went.

THE END

THE FIGHT SUMMARY:
TEN ROUNDS TO FREEDOM

THE FIGHT SUMMARY: TEN ROUNDS TO FREEDOM

ROUND 1
ABC's of Inner Boxing
Attacking Thought:
Identify the self-defeating thoughts you are using in the situation
Block the Attacking Thought:
Ask "Is this thought true? Where does this thought lead? Is that where I want to go?"
Counterpunch:
Replace the attacking thought with a productive thought

ROUND 2
A: It can't be done.
C: Think outside the box; see the problem from another angle.

ROUND 3
A: If I ignore the prices, I won't have to pay them.
C: If I ignore the prices, I'll pay even more in the long run!

ROUND 4
The Prayer of Epictetus
Lead me, Zeus and Destiny, whith ersoever I am appointed to go. I will follow without waverin g; even tho ugh I turn coward and shrink, I shall follow all the same.

ROUND 5
A: I'm a victim of events.
C: Assume that all events happen for my good. What benefit is hidden in this trial?

ROUND 6

A: I'm entitled to have whatever I want without having to work for it.

C: I am grateful for what I have and can earn what I want.

ROUND 7

A: Others should serve me.

C: I can help myself by helping others.

ROUND 8

A: He can't say that to me!

C: He has freedom of speech – he can say whatever he wants. In fact, I give him permission!

ROUND 9

A: I won't get caught.

C: I will get caught!

ROUND 10

A: I must worry and be anxious about events.

C: Be CALM. Some things are up to us, and some things are not up to us.

ADDITIONAL RESOURCES

The author drew primarily from two sources for the teachings of Epictetus, and in the book these sources are referred to collectively as the *Enchiridion*, which means handbook or manual. These two small but succinct books are recommended by the author for anyone interested in furthering their study of Epictetus:

The Handbook of Epictetus, translated by Nicholas P. White, 1983, Hackett Publishing Company.

A Manual for Living: Epictetus, A New Interpretation by Sharon Lebell, 1994, HarperSanFrancisco.

If you work with offenders and would like to provide a program similar to the one described in this book, contact us for information about *The Epicte tus S elf-Mastery Program: Helping Offenders Break Free of Criminal Attitudes*, a comprehensive sixteen-session program manual with activities, worksheets, and outlines by Jeff Traylor. An *Epictetus Club Discussion Guide* is available for teachers, librarians and others who would like to lead a discussion group about the book. On-site training is also available. Copies of *The Epictetu s Club* and the other materials are available through inquiry at: EpictetusClub@aol.com.

ABOUT THE AUTHOR

Jeff Traylor has a wealth of corrections experience, ranging from implementing the furlough program at the maximum security Ohio Penitentiary to serving as the cognitive skills instructor at a community based correctional facility. His experience also includes substance abuse counseling and program development, and he has worked in the psychological and social services departments in Ohio prisons. He is the creator of the Shoplifting Diversion Program that earned a national award from the National

Council of Community Mental Health Centers and was adopted in more than 30 U.S. cities. He has served on the faculty of the Michigan Judicial Institute and has trained hundreds of professionals ranging from parole officers to social workers. He earned his graduate degree from The Ohio State University and is the author of a series of Ohio travel books called *Life in the Slow Lane*.

THE EPICTETUS CLUB
REVIEW QUIZ

THE EPICTETUS CLUB REVIEW QUIZ

1. Epictetus was a:
    a. Race horse
    b. Greek philosopher
    c. Antidepressant drug
    d. Gang leader

2. According to Epictetus, we are upset by:
    a. Our childhood
    b. What other people say or do
    c. Our own thoughts
    d. Our past

3. The meetings of the Epictetus Club were held where?
    a. In a Greek restaurant
    b. In the Death House
    c. At the Courthouse
    d. At the Clubhouse

4. Before going to prison, Zeno was a:
    a. Pro boxer
    b. Plumber
    c. Drug dealer
    d. Truck driver

5. The men of the club were unable to solve the nine dots problem because they did not:
    a. Pay attention
    b. Think outside the box
    c. Have enough time
    d. Work together

6. Which of these is *not* a way that Zeno taught to handle being insulted?
   a. Like a rock
   b. Like a founding father
   c. Like a comic
   d. Like a wounded animal

7. Most offenders mistakenly think they will not get caught for their crimes. True or false?
   a. True
   b. False

8. One of the key thoughts that Zeno taught in handling stress was:
   a. Some things are up to us, some things are not
   b. It's better to yell than to hold it in
   c. I must control every situation
   d. If I worry enough, everything will be all right

9. Doc redeemed himself at Marion Correctional Institution by:
   a. Indirectly saving a woman's life by teaching the guards CPR
   b. Breaking up a fight between inmates
   c. Earning his GED
   d. Keeping a good institutional record

10. Instead of thinking that we should have whatever we want without having to work for it, it is better to think:
    a. I am grateful for what I have and can earn what I want
    b. Others should take care of me
    c. I should have it because others have it
    d. I'll get it too if I'm lucky

11. The group members learned that making excuses is like:
    a. Getting others to believe you
    b. Blowing a head gasket and losing power
    c. Getting away with something
    d. Being smarter than others

12. Animal's story about the back half of the dog meant that:
    a. There are always consequences for our actions
    b. Dogs shouldn't be allowed in parks
    c. If the tail is wagging, it is OK
    d. His dog shed too much

13. Don King told Zeno to "find the precious jewel hidden in the hair of that ugly and venomous toad," meaning:
    a. You can never find what you are seeking
    b. Find the benefit hidden in every trial
    c. People who speak meanly are like toads
    d. Ancient toads had hair

14. In the ABC's of Inner Boxing, A is the attacking thought, B is the block, and C is the:
    a. Consequence
    b. Change
    c. Counterpunch
    d. Conscience

15. Which of these did Epictetus say is most important?
    a. Having a lot of money
    b. Having a lot of time
    c. Having a lot of things
    d. Having a good purpose in your life

I have read this book and completed the quiz on my own (if required by judge, probation officer, counselor or other authority.)

Signature _____ Date _____